CLINGING

This book is a work of fiction. Names, characters, places, and incidents either are products of the author's imagination or are used fictitiously. Any resemblance to actual persons, living or dead, events, or locales is entirely coincidental.

Printed in Australia

Cover and internal design by Shawline Publishing Group Pty Ltd

First printing: March 2024

Shawline Publishing Group Pty Ltd

www.shawlinepublishing.com.au

Paperback ISBN 978-1-9231-0141-8

eBook ISBN 978-1-9231-0142-5

Hardback ISBN 978-1-9231-0184-5

Distributed by Shawline Distribution and Lightning Source Global

Shawline Publishing Group acknowledges the traditional owners of the land and pays respects to the Elders, past, present and future.

A catalogue record for this work is available from the National Library of Australia

CLINGING

BRUCE
RYAN

Also by Bruce Ryan

1936

Dedicated to Barbra Legge and her amazing family.
For my mother, Hirell, and sisters, Janet and Lyn, for their support.
With special thanks for early editing to Eleanor Stahl.

Chapter 1

DARK, SUNKEN EYES and a defeated countenance were how the three boys remembered their mother. Chelsea, London, England in the early 1800s was not an easy place to live with three sons under six and a worthless, drunkard husband. William had taken to the bottle in 1825 after the birth and death of their only daughter, Elizabeth, who was named after her mother.

The eldest of the boys, William, named for his father, was born in 1821, and Henry 1822. They remembered the night when their mother found Elizabeth blue in the crib. The sight of the little, perfect body, though lifeless, would stay in their memories until the end of their days. George had limited memory of the event, as he was very young at the time, but he did remember the image of her frail body.

The family had no money to send William and Henry to be educated, and though George, the youngest, started school in 1830, their miscreant father's trouble with the law made it impossible for him to continue. Elizabeth had used her family to make ends meet, borrowing from her mother, though her father had disowned her when she became pregnant with William, forcing her to marry his hapless father. She had also borrowed from her brother and sister, but there being no way for her to pay them back, all her bridges were finally burned.

Living in a two-room hovel, the boys all knew the violence of their father when drunk. When he began to rant, they would disappear to the outdoor toilet, which served four families. They all knew what would happen next. Their mother had always borne the scars and bruises. The old widow, Towton, who lived on the ground level of the adjacent building, once found them freezing in the outbuilding and gave them food, though she could spare little. This became a regular event in their lives while their father's drinking money lasted. Towton feared the violent man, as did all of the neighbours, and so could not take the boys in to protect them. She often brought old clothes out to them with the food, doing as much as she dared.

The boys had been told that their father fought in the street to make enough to service his bar tab, and many times, he had been arrested for stealing and other petty crimes. Most of the time, however, the witnesses refused to testify when they heard the record of the violent offender they were accusing. Finally, the law had its way, and in 1831, William Douglas was found guilty of assaulting an officer in the local army corps and was sent down for a term of three years.

Elizabeth succumbed to the dreaded consumption in 1832. This fate also befell her husband soon after. The boys stayed with Towton for some months, before she, too, was taken by the terrible disease. This was nothing new to the people of Chelsea, with one in five deaths being attributed to consumption or cholera at the time. None of the family members was in position to take the boys in, and soon, William and Henry were moved to a shoe factory, where they were put to work treading urine-fixed dye into leather.

George was taken to an orphanage in Yorkshire and never saw his brothers again.

Though the luck of the draw had conspired against the three, each worked hard and became a respectable member of their community. At twenty-five, William married Eliza, who was only fourteen, and immediately, they began a family. They had three children under the age of five when the bitterly cold winter saw all three youngsters in quick succession succumb to the awful influenza epidemic. The couple, though devastated by the loss, decided to start again. In 1855, William joined the East India Company's army. Rumours of an uprising had seen its army numbers increased by one hundred and twenty percent.

William was thirty-four when he arrived in India. Eliza and her twins, born shortly after William had shipped out, arrived just as the uprising began in 1856. In 1858, after the revolt had been supressed, the family decided to migrate to Australia. During preparations, Eliza found she was again with child. Agnes was born in 1858. Eliza was a sickly woman who found giving birth again more difficult than expected. Despite this fact, and the incredibly rough crossing to Australia, the family arrived together in early 1859.

Henry was lost to the family at that time, but later found to have been in India from the early 1850s.

George suffered through an unpleasant young life in the orphanage, and it is here that our story begins. The Dorothy Winterview Orphanage for Homeless Children was not as welcoming as the name made it sound. Once, it had been a great building designed as a private hospital. The rich socialite for whom the building had been renamed had donated it some thirty years earlier for its current use, perhaps to assuage some socio-economic guilt.

When George arrived, he became a whipping boy for the sadistic housemaster James Draper; this pitiful excuse for a human being would beat children terribly to ensure their obedience. Though often, he would thrash them for his own enjoyment. A doubled-up belt was his usual method of torture, but he would use his bare hands or feet if they were the only weapons available.

George had felt the weight of heavier blows when his father was 'under the weather', and if knocked down, would spring right back to his feet to be hit again. Many of his house companions revered him as the bravest in their midst, and all knew that while Draper was beating George, he was leaving them alone.

Infuriated by the strength of the boy's character, Draper took to striking him in the middle of the chest at the start of each day's work in the laundry, which was the only form of income the orphanage had, following the death of their benefactor several years earlier. This violence would take the wind right out of George, and Draper would stand over him, sneering, saying things like 'Not so smart now!' or 'I thought you were supposed to be tough?'

One morning in his second year at the orphanage, George decided to take things into his own hands. He placed a square cast-iron drain cover inside his shirt and tied it in place with several strips of bandage he had taken from the infirmary. This wasn't so well thought out, for though it had the desired effect of breaking two of Draper's knuckles, it also cut George's chest open and snapped two of his ribs. It served to enrage Draper even further. He backhanded George across the face and jumped on top of him, punching him with his undamaged fist. He almost certainly would've killed George, had another housemaster not intervened and dragged him away to the infirmary for treatment. George's friends carried him to a linen bale, where two of the older boys treated the bleeding and bandaged his ribs.

In the workhouse, the boys each had a quota of items they had to wash each day. Now the group divided George's share and started to work hard to cover that extra load. Draper did not return that day, having his hand set in a long plaster. One of the younger and more compassionate guards, Gibson, made sure that the boys were completing their quota. Many of the guards would give the boys a whack if they stepped out of line, but they never had the intent to severely injure a child.

George was quite tall, strong, and tough for his age, but this incident laid him low for several days. He was placed in the infirmary under the care of Mrs Marshall, the nurse, cook and laundry co-ordinator.

Marshall was one of the few pleasant adults the boys had contact with, and several girls helped her run the areas she controlled. When Draper returned to work, he was placed in the house for older boys; the rumour was that Mrs Marshall had complained about his treatment of some boys. This wouldn't have swayed the orphanage's board of governors had she not said that the purchase of bandages and the loss of work were affecting its bottom line. Gibson was placed in Draper's position, to the great relief of the boys.

While in the infirmary, George struck up a friendship with a beautiful blond-haired girl named Willow, who was one of Marshall's assistants. She was kind and gentle when changing his dressings and always spoke to him kindly, even though she was three years his senior.

They told each other of their former lives, and she explained that she had gained her name when she was five or six. Her father decided that she didn't look like a Gail, and her hair blew in the breeze like the foliage of a weeping willow. George was far too young to consider love, but he admired Willow, and over the next three days, they struck up quite a close relationship.

When George came back to his house, he was regarded as something of a hero, having rid them all of the terrible scourge that was Draper. The boys crowded around, keen to see the eighteen stitches across his midriff.

Martin Hyland was perhaps George's closest friend and was first to meet him when he was returned to the house by Willow. Martin, who was two years older than George, knew Willow; he'd been known to intentionally injure himself to visit her. He had already informed her that he was going to be her husband. As yet, she hadn't responded to his proposal, but they had kissed at their last meeting.

After greeting George and leading in three cheers for him, Martin turned his attention to Willow, offering to walk her back to her house.

'That won't be necessary,' she said, seeing the eyes of all the other boys on her, waiting for her answer.

'Perhaps not, but I will anyway.' Martin offered her his hand.

She took it and, as they exited the room, the group as one gave a knowledgeable *Ooh*. She and her suiter both blushed.

The walk was hardly that, as the houses faced each other across an open courtyard, which measured no more than forty yards. Willow's delivery into safety completed, Martin quickly began his recrossing. He noticed, skulking in the shadows at one corner of the yard, smoking an extremely long pipe, none other than Draper. He could tell Draper was watching him and increased his gait.

Draper strode to intercept him and grabbed him by the arm just yards from the door to his house. 'Tell your little mate Douglas I'll catch up with him.' Draper sneered and pushed Martin toward the door.

Martin rushed inside and, finding George surrounded by his admirers, rapidly recounted his meeting. The boys shot furtive glances at each other. They all knew what Draper was capable of.

'Well, there isn't much we can do about it. If we report him, he'll just call you a liar and deny everything,' George said.

'We should tell Mrs Marshall,' Martin suggested. 'At least she's honest.' He was supported by the rest of the group. George made no comment but nodded.

After a short time spent discussing other things that had happened during George's convalescence, the group prepared for church. Being Sunday, the entire contingent of boarders and staff were expected to twice march to the church, which was approximately two miles from the orphanage. There was no money for 'Sunday-best' clothing, and many of the garments were on their third or fourth hand-down, either from larger boys or those who'd perished in the infirmary. Saturday's wash had been conducted, and all had a clean change of clothes for worship. This was a great luxury as their work clothes were only washed every other week.

Willow seemed to glow in Martin's eyes, her face surrounded by her beautiful wind-swept hair. Martin was also blond and tall and thin for his age, though everyone was thin at the orphanage. Inmates weren't allowed to walk together in a 'co-ed' fashion as in some other schools. The boys were led by their three housemasters, the girls some twenty paces behind, led by their two mistresses. The rest of the staff, including the two gardeners and several housemaids, followed with Mrs Marshall.

After church, the children were allowed to walk calmly and respectfully around the churchyard and speak to each other in quiet tones, always under the eye of the ever-watchful staff. This was the only real social outing that the general populace were allowed.

Occasionally, a child was selected to go to some big house and become a possession of its master. For six years, if they were indentured as an apprentice, and sometimes for longer. If an owner hired an orphanage child for domestic duties, they would never really be compelled to name that child truly qualified. An upstairs housemaid, for instance, may always remain just that, if it was thought she wasn't comely enough to be seen by guests.

This was the best one could hope for, however. If not selected by the age of sixteen, one would be directed to the workhouse and there exploited mercilessly until some formal contract could be signed.

Though the orphanage was geared to make money to pay for its staff and upkeep, and to pay more-than-generous stipends to its board members, a need to show that the inmates were being educated was thinly adhered to, with all students under sixteen having lessons three afternoons a week in mathematics and English. These lessons were given by the housemaster, and George was excelling under Gibson's tutelage. He had a natural aptitude for mathematics, and though his English was raw when spoken, he could at least read and write basic sentences. Martin was also doing well at mathematics, though Gibson seemed to have given up on his English, once saying cruelly, 'If one sounds like a guttersnipe, one will be treated like a guttersnipe.'

In fairness, Gibson and most of the other housemasters had been hired as guards and had no formal teaching qualifications. The board of governors could therefore pay them as guards while covering the education program.

After one Sunday church service, Martin and Willow were observed holding hands on one of the wrought-iron benches around the parish hall. The housemistress who saw this rushed up to them and demanded that 'all expressions of an inappropriate nature cease at once'. The couple, who hadn't realised they were being watched, separated their hands and thought no more of the matter.

On return, both were called to the governor's office individually and berated for 'wantonly bringing the orphanage into disrepute'. They were banned from speaking to one another for a month.

This was a long time for Martin, who was smitten by Willow, his first love, and he resolved to break the order at his earliest convenience. George and all his housemates vowed to help them converse if possible. Each in his own way was proud of Martin's sally into the unknown realm of romance.

Gibson liked the boys in his house, and they, in turn, gave him little difficulty, knowing how much better off they were with Draper gone. That evening, Gibson spoke to Martin, telling him that Draper had pushed for a year of non-communication. Most of the other masters and mistresses had little problem with the incident, thinking it a very minor infraction, but Draper had lobbied hard for the ban, and the governor relented but lessened the parole period to one month.

'He's gunning for you, boy,' Gibson told him. 'Don't even look in her direction.'

'But, sir, we weren't doing anything wrong,' Martin pleaded.

Gibson raised a quizzical eyebrow. 'The rules on fraternisation are strict, as they must be, and you would both do well to observe them.'

Martin simply said, 'Yes, sir.'

Gibson stood and left. George had been in the room with several other boys, and though they'd been at a fair distance, they'd all heard the discussion.

'What are you going to do?' one of the group asked as they all rushed up to the bed where Martin sat.

'Not sure yet, but a month is a long time,' he answered.

'Just keep away for the month, and he won't be able to touch you,' George suggested sympathetically.

Martin nodded. He took what Gibson had said seriously, and the conversation ended as the bell for the evening meal rang. All knew that being late would see them going without food for the night and serving as dishwasher at its end, so their immediate response was guaranteed.

Chapter 2

FOR THE NEXT few days, Willow was not seen at meals or her usual work in the infirmary. Mrs Marshall said, when asked where Willow was, that she had developed a bad cold and was in bed to recover. Martin and George thought that this was just her way of staying out of Draper's view, but as several others fell sick over the next week and were also laid low, they began to believe the story.

On the fourth day, George took ill and was sent to the nurse for treatment. Usually, with an illness that was thought to be contagious, children were isolated in the infirmary for two to three days and given more hot drinks than usual. This was not done out of care for the ill, but for worry about the bottom line.

On his arrival, George caught a glimpse of Willow in a bed near the door of the girls' room, though she didn't see him. He resolved to try to visit her before leaving the infirmary.

George screwed up his face when the ill-tasting and smelling concoction that usually greeted sick inmates was served to him. Mrs Marshall laughed. 'It will do you good. Drink it all, and then get some rest.' She pointed to a bed in the corner.

He took the draught as instructed and could hardly believe how abhorrent it tasted. He coughed and spluttered, and Mrs Marshall laughed again.

Later in the day, Draper reported to Mrs Marshall and took the same concoction. George watched his ugly face grow even uglier as he swallowed it. The right side of his mouth split into two jowl lines rather than one as normal. This created a small island of flesh, which always seemed to be scab-ridden. No one was ever sure whether this was because he sliced the top off it every time he shaved or if it was irritated by the constant darting of his tongue as if to check it was still there. His greying hair was thick at the front and sides, with a shiny bald patch on the crown, appearing almost as a monk's cut. All in all, he was a most unappealing man.

He scowled at George as he passed. Although George thought Draper terrible in every way, he could never have foreseen the long-term effect he would have on all of their lives.

The next Sunday's walk to the church was the first time Martin saw Willow after their separation, and then only from a distance. Mrs Marshall was determined to keep them apart, so Draper would have no trigger point for his hostility. They did get to share a smile across the church once as they knelt to pray, and Martin watched her all the way back to the orphanage, as the girls were in front. George wasn't with the group; he was still in the infirmary. When all were released from the quadrangle to return to their houses, Martin made his way to where Mrs Marshall stood ushering the girls in through the door. She had made sure Willow was one of the first to go inside.

'Excuse me, miss,' he said. 'Could you tell me how George Douglas is?'

Before she could answer, Draper was at her shoulder. 'Is this young lout annoying you?'

'Certainly not. He's just enquiring about his friend's condition.' Mrs Marshall wasn't at all intimidated by the obnoxious man. 'He should be back with you tomorrow or the next day,' she told Martin.

'Thank you, miss,' Martin answered and began to walk across to his house.

Draper moved to his smokers' corner, scowling, and watched the boy until he was out of sight.

The next morning, George was returned to his house by Mrs Marshall, as she had no other place to put all the new cases of illness she'd received overnight. She instructed him to stay in his bed for one more day. He obeyed, as he didn't feel his recovery was complete.

Martin was delighted to have his best friend back. That evening, he reported that he'd seen Willow, though only for a few seconds, as she'd greeted her friends on their return from work. She had smiled at him from across the courtyard.

'She's so beautiful; I'll marry her one day.'

'If she's so beautiful, why would she look at you?' one of the boys asked mockingly. All present laughed, and Martin took a pretend swing at the offender.

'Only three weeks to go, and you can talk to her again,' said George. He could see the delight in his friend's face; Martin was truly smitten by Willow.

The weeks passed slowly. The boys kept their heads down and worked hard, as they usually did. Gibson had regular talks with Martin, suggesting he stay out of Draper's way, especially on the last Sunday of the ban. Martin hated Draper for this imposed separation and told Gibson how terrible he thought Draper was.

'You don't know the half of it,' Gibson replied. 'Keep your head down and your mouth shut.'

Martin nodded; he wasn't delighted about giving in to the thug, but he admired and respected Gibson.

The day in church came and went. Willow smiled at Martin across the pews, and he beamed back at her. They deliberately had no contact on the march home, and Martin retired to bed knowing the next day he was free to speak to Willow again.

In the morning, he was one of the first to make his way into the courtyard, ready for work. He paced up and down, waiting for Willow to show herself. For almost half an hour he waited, and most of the inmates were lined up, ready to leave, when Willow finally exited the house with Mrs Marshall.

It hadn't been the girl making him wait, but rather Mrs Marshall, who was determined to keep her safe. Martin slowly walked over to them and said, 'Good morning.'

Almost before he got the words out, Draper emerged from the shadows. Grabbing him by the shoulder, Draper swung him around and struck him across the face. 'You were warned, boy!'

Martin hadn't seen him coming and fell to the ground, narrowly being missed by Draper's second blow. Willow screamed, as did several other girls in her line.

'Mr Draper!' Mrs Marshall shrieked as he dragged the senseless boy to his feet. Martin was quickly knocked down again. 'Mr Draper, their restriction ended yesterday!'

She stepped between the man and the boy. He gave her a shove, and she fell heavily on her back. George rushed to Martin's aid and was also struck down.

Gibson had been locking the house door, but seeing the fracas, he ran at Draper, pushing him away from the fallen. 'Get a hold of yourself, Draper!'

Draper almost toppled but swung around and produced a knife from his belt. He had completely lost his senses. He lunged at Gibson, who dodged the blow and shouted, 'What are you *doing*?'

Draper aimed another backhanded blow with the knife. Gibson parried, but the follow-through struck Willow in the face as she went to assist Mrs Marshall. She fell, blood immediately covering her face and spraying onto the stricken woman. Gibson, through all the screams and cries of the children, could be heard saying, 'Drop it, man!'

However, his words tapered as he was struck in the chest, and he too fell bleeding to the cobbled surface. Martin had regained his feet and stared bewildered at the carnage around him. He had no time to react and was felled by a blow to his face.

The furore had drawn the attention of the gardener, who entered the courtyard with his hoe and immediately moved to protect the injured. Several other housemasters arrived, one saying, 'You'll be hanged, you fool!'

The wild-eyed Draper made another lunge and was struck hard by the gardener's hoe. This seemed to bring him to his senses. He dropped his blade and backed away.

'Get a doctor!' one of the masters shouted, and a subordinate ran from the courtyard. Draper recovered his knife, fled through the main entrance and disappeared.

Several of the older girls who'd been trained by Mrs Marshall began to treat the injured. 'Bring sheets and blankets,' one ordered and was soon obeyed.

They wrapped Willow in a blanket, as she wouldn't take her hands away from her face. Others rolled Martin and George, who were both unconscious, onto blankets and covered them. One of the girls started to pack Martin's wounded face with a white sheet, and soon the amount of blood flow was obvious. Two girls and several boys helped Gibson onto a blanket and staunched the wound on his chest.

Mrs Marshall lay groaning but wouldn't allow the many gathered around to move her. The attendants, however, covered her with several blankets to keep her warm.

Soon, the governor, Mr Graves, appeared, as one of the boys had run to his office and informed him of the incident. On seeing the carnage, he ordered one of the bystanders to go to the residence and bring his wife, who'd trained as a nurse.

Graves was essentially a kind man, and he showed his compassion by sitting next to Gibson and enquiring as to his condition. Gibson was coughing up blood and looked almost unconscious, but managed to answer, 'I'll be alright.'

Doubting this was true, Graves put more pressure on the right side of Gibson's chest, where the knife had obviously penetrated his lung. 'Hold on,' Graves said as Gibson began to lose consciousness, but soon he was unable to be roused.

Mrs Graves arrived, saw her husband with Gibson, and barked out her first order. 'Bring water and bandages from the main storeroom.'

Several girls rushed off to do her bidding. She moved to Gibson and pulled his shirt open to see the wound. Packing it again, she lay him down on his injured side and positioned two boys with their knees at his back so he was stable. She went to Willow and took her hands away from the wound on her face; it stretched from just above her right eyebrow down to her chin. Luckily, the blade had missed her eye, but it had penetrated her cheek all the way through, and the bone of her lower jaw was visible. Gently, Mrs Graves bandaged her head, only leaving her eyes and mouth uncovered.

Mrs Graves had thought the two boys to be dead, as they had been completely covered by the blankets. Now, George sat up, though he wasn't immediately sure what had happened.

'Lie down, boy,' Mrs Graves said. On seeing Martin's face, she took the least bloodied end of the sheet and cleaned the area around his cut. Unlike Willow's wound, it had been from an upward blow and had penetrated deepest under the jaw, slashing up the face and exiting at the cheekbone. Blood was still gushing from it, and she wrapped it in the same way she had for Willow.

Quickly, she checked George for blood, and seeing none, she told him to stay where he was. She moved back to Gibson, who rested in her husband's arms. She started to check the wound again but was replaced by the doctor, Newly, as he arrived in quite a fluster. He pressed a pinard horn to Gibson's chest. Though stethoscopes had been in use for some years, he thought of them as newfangled gadgets for which he had no use.

'Punctured lung,' he stated. 'Get him into a bed, no sheets, with the wound up.'

Several of the house managers lifted Gibson and headed toward the infirmary. Moving to Mrs Marshall, Newly asked what her injury was. 'Broken hip, I think, Doctor,' Mrs Graves answered.

Feeling the area and lifting Mrs Marshall's leg slowly, to her immediate discomfort, he quickly declared, 'Broken neck of the femur, more like it.' He looked to Mrs Graves. 'Have you a stretcher?'

'Yes.' She motioned some of the boys toward the office.

'Don't load her until I'm ready,' Newly ordered, as he moved to where Willow lay. At first, she wouldn't take her hands away from her face, but he raised his voice. 'This is no time to muck around, girl.' And she felt compelled to obey.

On her revealing the wound, he exclaimed, 'Good God almighty, who did all this?'

The question was somewhat rhetorical, and no one thought to answer. It seemed unthinkable that one man, in a matter of minutes, could've done so much damage.

'She needs to go straight to a table,' Newly ordered and turned his attention to the two boys. George was the nearest, and as he saw no blood yet, he asked what the problem was.

'My friend first,' George answered.

Newly rolled Martin toward him and saw his face; several of the nearest girls also saw and swooned, to be attended by their friends.

'This one has to be operated on too,' he told Mrs Graves. 'I'll need assistance.'

She nodded.

Returning to George, Newly said, 'Now you, boy?'

'Just my chest.'

After feeling it for a few seconds, Newly declared, 'Two or three broken ribs. He can go on a bed, but move him slowly.'

As two boys returned with the stretcher and placed it at Mrs Marshall's side, a night watchman arrived, asking what had happened.

Mr Graves, freed of Gibson, stood and said, 'Come with me.' He led the watchman into an office adjoining the infirmary.

Soon, everyone had been moved to their treatment areas, and only the children and a few housemasters were left in the courtyard. Many of the girls were crying, and all the boys grouped in one corner, planning what they would do if Draper returned.

In the office, Graves was explaining Draper's actions, how mad the man had become, and that he was a threat to the public at large. After their discussion, the officer hurried away. Graves went to where Newly was already operating on Gibson, who had regained consciousness. Newly called for a scalpel and had two of his helpers hold Gibson's arms as he cut into the lower edge of the wound to extend its length. Gibson tried to muffle his cries, but as he had had no painkillers of any kind, he made quite a bit of noise. His lung injury meant that it was not safe to administer ether, and morphine was also dangerous for one with large blood loss.

'Hold him,' Newly ordered, and Graves assisted the women, pinning Gibson's flailing arms. Having enlarged the hole enough, Newly inserted a pair of rib spreaders of his own design and drew the handles apart. In normal circumstances, this would've been an incredibly painful experience, but for Gibson, it was even worse, as the knife had damaged one of his ribs on entry. Now the rib gave way, breaking with a loud click and an accompanying scream. Within moments, Gibson had thankfully passed out again.

Newly didn't flinch. He continued, with the assistance of Mrs Graves, to clear the blood until he could see the wound in the lung; it was sucking in air but, surprisingly, bleeding very little. Quickly pulling the edges together, Newly began to stitch them. Less than a minute passed as he plied his trade, then he said to Mrs Graves, 'Give me a drainage tube. Can you close the wound?'

'Yes, Doctor,' Mrs Graves answered. On inserting the tube, he left to attend the next patient.

After making sure that Mrs Marshall had been positioned well and had no obvious internal bleeding, Newly moved to the table where several of Willow's friends were comforting her. Seeing her distress every time he attempted to touch her wounded face, he made a quick decision to use some ether to take her out of the operation, which he knew would be a terrible one.

George, from his position, could see the stitches pulling Willow's flesh to and fro, lit by the window behind. As he watched blood trickle down her cheek, he felt pity, he felt anger, but most of all, he felt sick.

Martin was on a table in the adjoining room. He attempted to sit up to see how things were going with Willow, but his loss of blood made him swoon, and he was unconscious for some time. When he came round, Newly was putting the last stich in his chin. He started for a moment, then remembered what had happened. He tried to ask how Willow was, but Newly said, in a cracked and cranky voice, 'Remain still.'

Newly drew the last stitch tight and clipped it off. After padding the eye, he bandaged Martin's head.

The doctor turned to Graves and began to give a summary of his patients. 'This one and the girl will need me to come every day and change their dressings; they were both very lucky not to have lost an eye. Both will have terrible scars, though.'

Graves nodded.

'Gibson here will also need daily bandage changes and watching twenty-four hours a day to see that the drain allows the blood to get away. If his condition falters, I need to know about it immediately.'

'Of course,' Graves agreed.

Newly continued as he passed George's bunk. 'This boy has several badly broken ribs and will need to lie still for at least a week, perhaps two. Now, as for Mrs Marshall, she'll need to be monitored. I may have to operate if the bone doesn't set, or if the femoral artery is threatened. In other words, I'll need to be here for a couple of hours a day, and someone will have to take charge when I'm not.'

'That would be me, Doctor,' Mrs Graves answered. Newly looked at her and nodded approval.

'I'll be back this afternoon and will stay overnight.' Collecting his bag and coat, he made for the door, followed by Graves.

'Thank you, Doctor Newly,' Graves began. 'About payment–'

'We need not talk about that now,' Newly said and strode out.

Draper was seen several times over the ensuing weeks but was not apprehended. Although the inhabitants of the Winterview Orphanage went about their duties as normal, several of the housemasters were encouraged to wear side-arms.

All of the injured parties had begun to heal. While George had contracted a bout of influenza, he had recovered and was back in the house with the other boys. Mrs Marshall had been moved back to her own bed but was still at least three weeks away from resuming her duties. Martin had taken to daily walks around the orphanage with the quickly recovering Gibson; he'd tried to communicate with Willow, but she always turned her head away for fear of someone seeing her scar. Although it was still heavily bandaged, she continually covered her face with either her hands or a blanket. She would see no one and talked only to one of the girls who was helping nurse her.

Overall, it was a quiet time. Everyone was used to hard work and to some extent missed it, though the shovelling of coal into the wash-house boiler was not a job that any would've volunteered for in a hurry.

Three weeks after the incident, it was announced that Mrs Marshall was to travel to Kent to convalesce and she would be taking Willow with her. Martin again tried to communicate with Willow before she left, but she would not allow it. George, seeing the sadness this brought to his friend, attempted to intervene by visiting Mrs Marshall.

Knocking tentatively, he received a sprightly 'Come in.'

He opened the door and found Mrs Marshall in the rough wheelchair that had been constructed for her out of old and disused chairs as she was never going to fit into the standard children's size that the orphanage possessed.

'Well, Mr Douglas?' she questioned, with some humour in her voice.

'Sorry, ma'am, I was just hoping to enquire about your health.'

'My health, indeed? I thought you may have come to see Willow.'

'... Ah, that too,' he answered. He had never understood her humour, and was never sure if she was serious.

'She's in the other room, packing.' Mrs Marshall's bosom heaved as she waved her hand toward the bedroom. He looked at her for approval, and she nodded, so he entered and found Willow sitting on the floor, trying to close a suitcase.

'May I help?' he asked.

Willow hadn't heard him coming. She quickly dragged her shawl around her face, saying, 'No, thank you,' in a very timid voice.

'Martin is missing you.'

'I can't,' she said quietly.

'But it's not fair. He blames himself for what happened.'

'I don't want to see him like this.' She sounded as though she might cry.

'He just wants to talk to you,' George reassured her.

'I can't,' she sobbed, and though he could only see her eyes, he could tell how distraught she was. He went to give her a hug, but she flinched away. He felt impotent; he could help neither of his best friends.

'I'm sorry.' Slowly, he rose from the side of the bed and walked from the room.

'It will take time, dearie,' Ms Marshall said, as he passed her silently and departed.

Two hours later, the horse-drawn coach was loaded with what seemed all of Mrs Marshall's belongings. Just before it left for the railway station, Willow, with her face covered, rushed out and got into the coach, keeping her gaze low.

Martin was in the yard with many of the children. He spoke her name. She gave him a fleeting glance, then covered her eyes. The horse, given a tap, responded, and Willow was gone.

The boys heard some months later that Mrs Marshall's injuries had not mended well, and she and her sister had moved back to their ancestral home, taking Willow with them.

Martin never forgot Willow, but she was gone.

Chapter 3

GIBSON MADE A remarkable recovery and was back at lessons within three weeks. This was a godsend for George. He had a thirst for knowledge, and though he quickly surpassed Gibson's level in English and was rapidly soaking up all knowledge he had of mathematics, George worked hardest on map-making, the field in which Gibson's family had decades of experience.

George knew he owed Gibson a debt he could never repay. That debt became even more life-altering when, after studying hard for some years, the seventeen-year-old George was apprenticed for five years to a cartographer named George Bradshaw, Gibson's uncle, who'd taken over the family practice when Gibson's father passed away. Bradshaw took an immediate liking to the boy and asked for another to assist in the print shop. George suggested Martin, and within three months, they were sharing a small room at the workshop in High Street. Both now earned a wage, and though most of the money was taken back for bed and board, they felt they'd made a huge step forward from such humble beginnings.

In 1846, the boys migrated to Australia, assisting in the setup of Bradshaw's business in Sydney. By 1854, George had acquired land in Baulkham Hills, an outer suburb of Sydney, supplying the early city with vegetables, milk, mutton, and wool. George married Sarah

Williams, a tall, dark-haired beauty, in 1855. They had the first of their children, Sam and James, in 1858. Though no one would have expected it, the twins had incredibly striking red hair; a throwback, Sarah thought, to her grandfather.

Neither George nor his brother William was aware that the other had ended up in Australia.

In 1860, George's future, and that of his family, was secured when he purchased land near Bathurst in the Sofala area. Here, the land was even richer on the unfarmed banks of joining rivers. The paddocks were on rolling hills rising to the west, thus protecting the area where he'd decided to build a cabin. With Martin's assistance, a small but comfortable four-room hut was built overlooking the point where the two rivers met. The family and 'Uncle Martin' became well known and respected in the area.

George was only thirty-six and already a wealthy man, but he was ambitious and had plans for so much more. With two hundred acres of government-gazetted land, he began by running cattle and, through several good years, amassed a large herd of more than one hundred head.

The weather, they now found, was fickle, and not always conducive to the running of cattle. In 1862, the first year of a five-year drought, George looked to sell his holdings in Baulkham Hills to consolidate his position. A much larger sum than he'd expected was paid, and he acquired another two hundred acres of prime land in the small community of Brucedale, where their current holding lay.

The drought continued to bite. Although other farms went out of business, George's decision to diversify into sheep, which use much less water, was his saving grace.

When the rains came again, it was in a spring rush that washed away roads and saw bridges either destroyed or moved from their foundations. The twins were now nine years old and fairly independent. They were good riders and, having lived in the country all their lives, they were both adept at surviving in the bush.

Two days after the heaviest rain had ceased, Martin, George and the two boys rode out to judge the condition of the sheep flocks and bring as many as possible back into the paddocks nearest to the homestead, so they could be protected if the waters continued to rise. It was a long, hard day in the saddle, and many times, the riders had cause to get down to free sheep caught in fences or stuck in mud. They had separated to cover ground more quickly, with George instructing the twins to return to the homestead well before sunset.

Anxiously, James, George and Martin sat on the front veranda, waiting for Sam to return. Sarah continually moved from the kitchen to the front door to see if her boy had arrived. George continually reassured her, but after darkness fell, he and Martin resaddled their horses to go and search for Sam.

Hours later, Martin came upon the boy's horse drinking at a waterhole. Although he immediately began to shout and fired two shots from his rifle, there was no reply. After fifteen minutes, George came riding up in answer to the pre-arranged signal, and the two began to search the area on foot, looking for the smallest sign of Sam.

The sun rose, and there was still no Sam, no tracks to follow, no footprints from which they could deduce where the horse had wandered from. They returned to the homestead in the hope that he'd found his way back. James and Sarah met them, and though she looked expectantly into George's eyes, no words were spoken; a simple shake of his head communicated the situation.

The two men dismounted, and James led their exhausted steeds, along with his brother's, to the barn. There, he unsaddled, fed and watered them.

'We'll go out again in two hours,' George told him. 'Have the other two horses ready.'

Sarah had prepared a large meal for the men, and they sat in front of the open fire, drying as they ate and drank several cups of extra-sweet tea. Soon, both slept where they sat, and Sarah left the room, allowing them the two hours to rest. Few words had been spoken, but they all knew that the longer Sam was missing, the worse his condition must be. When George and Martin struck out again, Sarah and James were both in tears, waiting with the gravest fears. James had wanted to join them, but there was no other rested mount, and George wanted him to stay with his mother.

The men again separated as they headed to the north-western boundary of the property. George rode quickly, as he planned to cover a large area, rather than trying to track in the impossible conditions.

Returning to the homestead just after dark, both men dropped from their mounts, totally exhausted. Indeed, James had to assist his father into the house. All knew that it wasn't possible to go out again in the dark with the rain still pouring steadily.

The mood was grim as they sat around the large family table in the kitchen, trying to eat the meal Sarah had prepared. Sarah didn't cry, though her eyes were red from the tears she'd shed when on her own. George took her hand, then James's with his other. Sarah in turn reached for Martin, and James completed the link.

'We thank you, Lord, for this, thy bounty,' George said, 'and pray for the safe return of our son and brother, Samuel. We ask this in your name. Amen.'

The other three repeated the amen, and though the prayer had been completed, Sarah and George didn't let go of each other's hands.

Immediately after the meal was finished, they all retired to their beds. While fear for Sam's safety was upmost in their thoughts, exhaustion soon forced them all to sleep.

The rains continued to rage. Lightning heralded the obligatory crashing thunder. Strange as the human mind is, none of this woke the family; however, the dripping of a single leak, which had appeared just outside James's bedroom door, had roused him, and it was driving him to distraction. Finally, he got out of bed as a streak of morning sunlight lit the gap between his curtains. He went to investigate the leak and found a large puddle, with the drips quickening. Moving to the kitchen, he found a bucket full of last evening's washing-up water and hurried to the front door to empty it. He cast the contents out into the garden and, turning to return to the house, was confronted by a huge Aboriginal warrior, his almost-naked body gleaming in the sunlight. The rain still fell, though more as a mist now, and the resulting glow highlighted the man and his troop eerily.

James was so shocked that he screamed. He wasn't frightened of Aboriginal men; he had seen them before, but the suddenness of their arrival was enough to unsteady anyone.

The man raised his hand to calm the situation. Both George and Martin burst through the front door, each clutching his rifle. A front window opened, and another muzzle, that of a double-barrelled shotgun, became visible.

George immediately realised that three guns wouldn't stop the number of warriors and family in front of him. He placed his, slowly and carefully, against the wall and signalled to Martin and Sarah to do the same. 'Yamandhu marang?' he asked, in very poor Wiradjuri, the language of most Aboriginal groups in this area. He had picked up a few words when dealing with workers and trackers over the years.

The leader of the troop nodded.

'James, drop your head and back away,' George instructed, and the boy obeyed, moving to a position behind his father.

The obvious leader of the troop took a step forward and said, 'Wurrmany – gunya.' He signalled by opening the palm of his right hand.

'Sorry,' George said, not understanding.

The man repeated it slowly. 'Wurrmany – gunya.' Then, he said, 'Son... Home.' Stepping aside, he signalled to his band, and they divided to reveal Sam lying in a litter.

Sarah screamed and ran from the house, straight past the men. She threw herself on to her knees beside her unconscious son. The man still stood before George and said, 'Broken, broken,' patting his upper thigh.

George nodded. 'Thank you.' He extended his right hand. The man paused for a moment, then, switching his spear from his right to his left hand, took George's, and they shook slowly.

The warrior said a few words, and the blankets were removed from Sam. Two women lifted him, and Martin came forward to carry him into the house. Sarah hugged the two women in turn, and the troop turned and began to walk away.

'Thank you!' George shouted. 'If ever we can repay you... Thank you.'

Turning, he found that James was still behind him, and they embraced and made their way to the house. George stopped at the front door and turned to see the last of the Wiradjuri passing through the open gate. None of them looked back, and his wave went unseen.

Chapter 4

SAM'S RECOVERY WAS slow. He had fallen down a large embankment and broken his femur in at least two places. The swelling and bruising took nearly two weeks to go down, but the pain in placing any weight on the limb remained.

James ran around him, doing jobs and making sure that he was comfortable. Although they fought like cats and dogs at times, his feeling of loss when Sam was missing had been so terrible that he wasn't going to allow it to happen again. Sam was enjoying the attention, and that of his mother, who made his favourite foods and sat with him for hours, doting over her 'darling boy', as she had taken to calling him.

James, Martin and George had brought all of the sheep in from the outlying areas of the farm and penned them near the house, away from the water, which ran many yards over the riverbanks. In some places, the two rivers had joined to create one sheet of water miles wide.

This isolation is something that farmers know only too well. There was little to do but mend the roof and farm tools and tend to the gardens when the rain stopped. The sheep were more pampered than usual, with all manner of injuries being treated and hand-feeding ensuring their wellbeing.

For almost five weeks, they were marooned as if on a desert island. Sam's leg mended to some extent, though the bone hadn't set straight. He was walking, slowly, but his limp was extremely noticeable. George had promised to take him to the surgeon at Bathurst when there was safe passage.

Sam regularly spoke of the kindness of the Wiradjuri troop who had rescued him. The men had found him first and waited until the women and elders came up to move him. He expressed admiration of the leader, who had lifted him into the litter without help, to make the movement as smooth as possible. One of the old women had treated him, fed him, and held him to her throughout the night under a lean-to, keeping his body temperature from dropping.

The boy had never been so close to Aboriginal people, and he was delighted that he had been able to understand them, though he knew nothing of their language. He did also mention the fact they were naked. He'd felt some discomfort from this, and from when he'd had to go to the toilet himself. George had reassured him that this was the way they lived, and that it was natural for him to feel uncomfortable.

George also continually spoke of getting along with the local tribesmen. 'They went to a lot of trouble to help you, Sam, and didn't ask for anything in return. They showed great honour and kindness, which they aren't usually given credit for.'

'I would like to learn their language,' Sam said.

'Me too,' James added.

'I'm not sure that's possible, but it's a goal that could hold you in good stead in the future,' George conceded.

When the first full day without rain came, George spent time with the boys at the wood pile behind the house, breaking up logs to the size most practical for use in their fires. He also took the chance to share the little knowledge he had of the Wiradjuri language. The boys enjoyed the time with their father, listening and learning.

Martin was as they'd always found him: reticent to be involved in anything where he had to converse with other people. Though he'd had extensive surgery on his scars, time and age had turned his face to a parchment on which all the lines were visible. He loved the family as if it were his own and would've done anything for them. There were times, however, when that was not enough, and his thoughts turned to his only love, Willow.

Though many years had passed, he thought of her ever more regularly. He wondered what had happened to her and where she was now. He sometimes made secret plans to go and search for her, but these came to nothing, as he doubted his ability to function if he was away from George for long.

Aware that he was viewed by anyone who met him as at least a ruffian, and often so much worse, Martin did not leave his place of safety often. He travelled to Bathurst with George to buy supplies but was rarely seen in public with Sarah or the boys. The three of them often tried to encourage him to visit the town with them, but he felt that his presence would only harm their reputation.

Like any man, though, Martin had the usual desires and needs. On occasion, he'd visit the women of a certain house on one of the ever-growing town's slightly less busy streets. These visits would happen only a few times a year, as money was tight, and he had such guilt afterwards that he would try to refrain. He'd had some very unpleasant times in his late teens when under the influence of alcohol and had decided that this brought the worst out in him. Now he acted as a virtual teetotaller, only having a little whisky if he developed a cold.

The boys engaged him in his only social outlet, cards. They would play as often as they could. Poker, blackjack and, when four players were available, five hundred. During this game in particular, he would let down his guard and feel like the boy at the orphanage again, with the friends whom he'd grown up with, and who had not reacted to the change in his looks after the terrible event with Draper.

It was while they were playing at the large oak kitchen table that Sarah and George entered to announce there would soon be another mouth to feed in the Douglas household. This surprised everyone, none more than Sarah herself, as she and George had tried for years after the boys were born for another child. Perhaps the extra time together during the floods had been more fruitful than they expected.

The two boys hugged their mother, and Martin shook George's hand warmly. George took a decanter of port from the top of the kitchen cabinet and poured everyone, even the boys, a small drop with which to celebrate the news. Sam and James both reacted by screwing up their noses at the first taste, though they both finished the offering quickly, knowing this first time was very special in their parents' eyes.

The boys left the adults to celebrate and promised to go and stable the horses for the night. George and Martin sat either side of Sarah on the hand-built couch in front of the fire. They had refilled their glasses, though Sarah declined. They were certainly doing well enough to bring up another baby, and all three loved children. They discussed whether the house would be big enough and decided to add another bedroom next to Sarah and George's. They all glowed as bright as the embers of the fire.

Sam and James gave the three horses used during the day a wash and rubdown. They were part of the family's livelihood, but also, both boys loved animals and spending time with them.

James, finishing the first horse, his father's, led the beautiful bay stallion into the barn and secured his stall, serving him a large bucket of oats and placing the daily allowance of hay at his feet. Sam brought the second horse through the door. As he entered the next stall, they both heard a sound as if someone was groaning.

The noise startled them both, and they stopped to see if it would be repeated. Soon came the sound of movement at the far end of the feed hay, which was piled beyond the four horse stalls.

James grabbed the nearest tool, a baling fork, and they crept along the dirt floor, trying not to make a sound. When they neared the end of the hay, James raised his hand to halt his brother, then on his fingers counted to three, and they both jumped into the open space. What they saw almost made them jump back as quickly.

A large Aboriginal man lay on the hay; he was bleeding from wounds over most of his body. Though he started at the boys' entrance, it was obvious he was in no condition to move.

'Get Mother,' James ordered, and Sam obeyed. James had always been the better at managing problems, and Sam had no problem conceding his authority in any dangerous situation.

Soon, the three adults joined them in the barn. Though the injured man was obviously scared, there was nowhere for him to go. Sarah soon set to work closing as many of his wounds as she could, bathing the worst of the injuries with water brought by Martin and bandaging them with old sheets she kept for just this type of event.

Sam had gone to the hall cupboard to retrieve the material and brought an old blanket as well. James spoke quietly to the man and washed his face to cool him as his mother did the painful work.

'This is a gunshot wound,' she said to the two men, who glanced at each other and nodded. 'And these look like whip marks.'

Examining the man's lower legs, Martin said, 'He's been dragged by a horse as well.'

As James wiped the man's beard, he flinched again, and the boy said, 'Oh, God... his neck.' As they all looked, he lifted the beard to reveal a terrible mark around the man's neck.

'Someone's tried to hang him,' the boy said in a horrified voice.

'No, he has been tied and led by the neck like a horse.' George shook his head in disapproval. 'No man deserves this kind of treatment.'

Martin also shook his head, and Sarah shed a tear, though she did not stop treating his wounds for a moment.

By the end of the task, the man had fallen into unconsciousness. Sarah, covering him with the blanket, said, 'I've done everything I can; now his fate rests with the Almighty.' She stood, and the three adults began to move to the barn door.

'Someone should stay with him.' James remained sitting next to the stricken body on the hay.

'I'll stay too,' said Sam and moved to his brother's side.

Sarah looked to George. As she did, Martin, seeing the worry in her eyes, intervened. 'I'll stay with them. We may need some blankets, though.'

George nodded, and he and Sarah walked from the shed toward the house. Before they could reach it, though, three rough-looking men on horseback rode up.

'We're looking for a black who escaped the stockade,' one of them said.

'We haven't seen anyone,' George answered quickly.

'Begging your pardon, sir, but seeing how your wife is covered in blood, we might just have a look for ourselves,' the second rider said.

'Begging your pardon, but I don't think so,' Martin said, striding out from the shed while closing one of the double-barrelled shotguns which were kept there for emergencies.

'We've been attending to an injured horse. You have no business here,' George said, as Sam clicked the other shotgun and stepped into the light.

Seeing that they couldn't bully the family, the first rider changed tack. 'Sorry, sir, we didn't mean to alarm you all, but this man was caught cattle rustling on Mr Sheffield's three-mile. He could be dangerous to you and your family.'

'I can't see one man without a horse rustling too many cattle,' Martin said.

'Well, he was there for some reason, and he might be dangerous,' the man answered with a sneer.

'Well, you better go and find him before he does something,' George said sarcastically. He didn't know any of the men but knew very well the Mr Sheffield they had mentioned.

Sheffield owned huge swathes of land in and around Napoleon Reef and Raglan, and further west. He had a reputation which suggested that he operated outside the law. However, none of the mud had stuck.

The three men looked at each other for a moment, and the first motioned with his head. They turned their horses to go, and the first man said, 'Mr Sheffield will hear that you wouldn't help us.'

'Good. I shall call on your boss and let him know that his men were so rude,' said George, determined not to allow this bully to get the last word.

Martin stayed on watch, fearing that the men hadn't been wholly deterred and that they may come back. Sam stood with him. Though he was young, he did know how to use a shotgun and was more than ready to protect his family and the man who lay in the barn. James had remained with the injured man and continued to wipe his brow as he perspired in his stupor.

Sarah and George went to the house. George soon returned with blankets and his favourite rifle. He had the same thought as Martin – they may not have seen the last of the riders.

The night passed without further incident, though George and Martin took turns on watch. The injured man awoke several times and started at his unfamiliar surroundings. Each time, James or Sam was there to reassure him and give him water. By morning, all four felt tired but satisfied. The man was safe.

Around sunrise, they smelt the household oven at work. Before long, Sarah arrived with two loaves of freshly cooked bread and a dish of butter. The family lived simply but ate like kings, as Sarah was from a family of wonderful cooks.

The injured man woke, and though he was unsure of his surroundings again, he accepted a small piece of bread fed to him by Sam. His wide-eyed expression filled Sarah with delight, and she offered more. He could barely lift his head but, assisted by Sam, was able to polish off several pieces.

'We'll need to go and visit Sheffield and let him know we won't be pushed around,' George said to the two adults.

'Do you think that's safe?' Sarah asked, taking his arm.

'Safer than letting it stew.'

'I think we have to go,' added Martin, and they all nodded in agreement.

The boys were told to keep their shotguns close during the day, and Sarah had several rifles and a pistol loaded and at hand. They moved the injured man into the rear room of the house, and made him comfortable, though he would not lie on the bed. He ended up on the floor, covered with bedding.

The two men brought several buckets of water into the house and said that all the doors and windows should be locked and barred when they left, with no one needing to venture outside.

The ride to the Sheffield spread was uneventful. In the midafternoon, Martin climbed out of his saddle and opened the gate under a large, curved sign which read simply 'Sheffield'.

They rode for almost another mile before they came to the ostentatious Georgian-looking house. A group of five men were at an outbuilding and came to 'greet' the two riders.

'Mr Sheffield?' George asked, addressing the best-dressed of the men.

'Yes, can I help you?' returned the man.

'My name is George Douglas, and I am your neighbour. I–'

Sheffield interrupted. 'Ah, yes, my son said you were not happy with his approach last night. Leave your horses and come inside, and I'll see if we can't be a bit more neighbourly.' He turned, not expecting an answer, and entered the large, hand-carved front doors of the house.

No sooner had George and Martin followed him through the door than they were attended by a housemaid, who insisted on taking their coats. The entrance was grand for a colonial house, being lined with plaster-panelled walls adorned with portraits of questioning forbears, whose height was so arranged that their disapproving eyes looked down on the visitors.

Sheffield threw open the double doors at the right side of the hall and bade the two men follow him into the majestic library, which was obviously also meant to impress. They looked around in wonder; this was an opulence which they had not expected, even from the richest man in the region, if not the colony. Twelve-foot ceilings were quite a rarity, and all three external walls had huge bay windows positioned to take advantage of the afternoon sun. All of the walls were covered with books, and the room was artificially lit by several large ornate kerosene lamps. A mounted marble sculpture of Paris stood in a running pose, on one foot, on a pedestal in a corner. Balancing this was a large fern in a jardinière of a rich blue and gold Chinese dragon design. The whole room would've been thought a vulgar display of new money in England, but in the young colony of Australia, it was even more bizarre.

The visitors were dragooned into following the shelves covered with thousands of tomes to the only other extravagance: a life-size portrait of the owner.

'Do you like books, Mr Douglas?' he asked, completely ignoring Martin.

'Yes,' George answered, striving in vain not to seem over-impressed.

'Oh, I never thought – can you read?' he asked in a condescending tone.

'Of course, but I'm not used to seeing so many books anywhere other than in a library.'

'Please make yourself at home.' Sheffield motioned to the four large leather reading chairs in one bay window. George and Martin sat down, and he continued, 'How are we to put this unfortunate incident behind us?'

'It was unfortunate but hardly an incident. I'm sure there was no ill intent, but it did come across as ill-mannered,' George answered. He had learned to play these word games while working in the map-making business, where he'd had to deal with many of these 'nose lifters', as he liked to call them.

'They were chasing a very dangerous man and felt that they were only protecting your family,' their host commented.

'I'm sure we can look after ourselves, but it is gratifying to think there are others offering to help,' George said. 'Did you catch this dangerous man? What was his crime?'

'No, as yet we have not seen the vagabond, but we will catch him eventually,' Sheffield answered.

'And his crime?' George asked again.

'Trespassing with intent, my learned colleague,' the other answered, feigning that he was in court. He paused, and then said, 'We have to stick together out here, you know.'

'In what way?' George asked.

'Well, these blacks can't be trusted,' came the answer, which he had expected.

'We haven't had any trouble with them; in fact, they saved my boy's life when he had a bad fall from his horse earlier in the year,' George countered.

'If you let them in, they will take everything you have and kill everyone.'

A long, awkward pause ensued, and was only broken when Martin said, 'We do wish to be good neighbours.' He could see the advantages of keeping a dialogue open. He had witnessed the damage men like this could do.

'Yes, I would think your boss would understand that,' Sheffield said dismissively.

'Martin is an equal shareholder in our selection,' George said, his eyes narrowing.

'Oh, really?' the man answered, in an incredulous and almost sarcastic way.

'We did our time together as cartographers and indeed ran the colony's foremost cartographic and printing company for some years.'

'Well, it just goes to show you can't judge a book by its cover,' Sheffield scoffed.

'No, certainly not.' George suggestively looked around at the salubrious surroundings.

Sheffield glared at them, having thought they would kowtow to a better man. It was as if they thought of themselves as equals.

'I shan't keep you any longer, then,' he said.

Martin and George stood and nodded as he showed them to the door. As a parting comment, he said, 'Watch out for those blacks.' He gave a little laugh.

'We'll watch out for all scoundrels,' George said. Neither man offered his hand, and the door was shut behind them. The housekeeper ushered them back to the front hall, returned their belongings, and then closed the grand door behind them.

'Well, that wasn't a very pleasant meeting,' Martin said, as they gathered their horses from the water trough.

'What a mongrel of a man,' George answered.

'Yes, but it can't help to antagonise him.'

'Surely you don't think I should've agreed with him?'

'No, but he is dangerous.'

George just nodded as they headed back to the front gate.

Over the next few weeks, the boys helped the warrior to convalesce. They found that his name was Jaiemba, to the best of their knowledge, and he was Wiradjuri. He said very little else unless pushed, though he was getting used to the family and clearly liked the two boys.

The time eventually came when Martin thought Jaiemba would be well enough to join his troop and spoke to him in a very broken version of his language. 'You go to your own family now.'

Jaiemba studied him, and said in English, 'No one left. Gone, gone.'

Martin tried to extract from him what he would like to do, where he would go, but there seemed no way of asking that question. Martin felt pity for his terrible loss, his whole family structure murdered. With a worried look, Martin walked into the house and found Sarah and George seated on the lounge in front of the fire. They both immediately picked up on his demeanour.

'What's wrong, Martin?' questioned Sarah.

'I was talking to Jaiemba about what he would do when he leaves here.' He paused. 'He doesn't understand me very well yet, but he says that all of his family are gone.'

'Well, perhaps he can catch up with them?' she answered.

'Not that kind of gone,' Martin said, dropping his eyes.

'You don't mean... *dead*?'

He nodded. 'It seems so.'

'We can't just turn him out,' Sarah said, looking to George.

'We need to handle this well.' George rubbed his forehead as he pondered the possibilities. 'If we turn him out, they'll catch and kill him, but we can't keep him here either.'

'Get the boys to find out where his people come from. Maybe they can be found in bigger numbers out west,' Martin said.

'How will that help?' Sarah asked.

'If there's a mob he could fit in with, we could get him out there,' Martin answered.

'How do you propose we do that?' George asked.

'We could put a false floor in the cart and load it up with supplies, so he's fully covered,' Martin suggested, and his companions nodded. 'Finding a troop could be our biggest problem.'

The boys agreed to try and find out if Jaiemba had a wider family, or if other Wiradjuri may take him into their troop. James had picked up the most Wiradjuri language, so he started the questioning, though Sam stayed with him, dressing the last wounds Jaiemba had which still needed treatment.

From what James gathered, the troop which contained Jaiemba's family had been ambushed, and all but him had been killed. He shed quiet tears as he told James how the riders just rode up, shooting.

James also fought back tears but was determined to find out more about the tribe. He knew that the Wiradjuri were the predominant tribe in the area, and that they ranged over a large part of the western area of the country.

Jaiemba, when coaxed, told James that he had a sister still alive who lived in the far west. He said he thought most troops would turn him away as they had more than enough mouths to feed. James asked if his sister's troop would be a possibility if he could get to them. He answered in an uncertain way but at least did not say no.

The boys reported back to the adults, and they all sat down to work out a way for them to get Jaiemba far enough west to be safe.

'The cut-out wagon would work for a short trip, but if we're talking about several days, it would be too rough,' Martin said.

'If we could get him out past Bathurst, it might be safe for him to ride up on top. It's really all about hiding him from Sheffield's men,' George said. 'It's none of their damn business why we're taking a loaded wagon out west.'

'Do we need to take it loaded?' Sarah asked. 'What if you brought the boys? They could sit on mats in the back and cover the false compartment.'

'Yes, that sounds like it could work.' George considered this and then said, 'But I don't like leaving you alone for that long.'

'I can handle the shotgun,' she assured him.

'What if I had Mrs Haynes and her daughters come and stay for a couple of days?' George put forward, thinking on his feet.

The Hayneses owned an adjoining property to the north, and Mrs Haynes and her two daughters were considered the finest dressmakers in the district.

'You could do with a new Sunday dress,' George told her.

Three days later, the wagon set out with four obvious passengers and Jaiemba hidden from sight. James very soon went to sleep, and they travelled for some time with only the sound of the wagon and the occasional neigh of the two horses.

Passing through Bathurst, they saw several people they knew and acknowledged with a hand gesture or nod of the head, intent on getting out on the open plains again without stopping. This achieved, in the early afternoon, they found a secluded area off the rough track, went about their ablutions, and ate the fine lunch which Sarah had packed for them.

Jaiemba was freed from his safe hold and given food and water. When asked, he intimated that even though the space was tight, it was not too uncomfortable.

After the horses had been watered and had a short rest of about forty minutes, the party got back on the road. George and Martin would've normally given them a longer break, but carrying Jaiemba instead of a load, the animals showed no signs of distress.

At around five o'clock, Martin drove the cart off the road and positioned it under a huge spreading eucalypt. The tree would have been more than a hundred years old and created some bare earth areas out to its drip line, which was mostly covered by its own fallen leaves. Large slabs of bark also lay around its base, and along with fallen branches which the boys collected, these soon roared into a beautiful campfire, ready for preparing the evening meal and for providing the night warmth.

A small tent was erected in which Martin and George were to sleep, and a canvas cover was strapped to the back of the cart to shelter the boys and Jaiemba. The early evening turned a little cold, and a light wind came up from the south, encouraging them all to linger by the fire for several hours before retiring.

During the night, the wind dropped, and they were met by one of the freezing white frosts for which the area was renowned. James, first to rise, piled wood on the fire to rekindle it. Flames lit the area to as far as ten feet. He was warm.

Soon, the others joined him, one at a time, and a sumptuous breakfast of over-cooked ham and eggs was prepared. The horses were happily standing by a small creek, where they had obviously taken their fill. Much of the grass within their reach had been eaten or at least flattened.

Since passing Bathurst the previous day, they had seen few travellers, and those only from a distance. This second morning was the same. A stagecoach rattled past with virtually no recognition, and a small Aboriginal family group were seen in the distance on a hill about half a mile from the track. They stopped and observed the group with the wagon and then disappeared into the bush without trace.

Getting close to a troop in this area seemed as though it would be a very difficult task.

They crossed many creeks and rivers in several different places, with little or no difficulty. Then, as if fate were telling them something, the wheels sank. The horses, though they gave their all, could not budge the vehicle.

It came as a surprise to Martin, who was driving. The boys hopped down into the cold water first and found that at its deepest point, it was no more than three feet to the top of the mud. The surface held them, for the most part, but quickly gave way when they added any force to the wagon. Sam replaced Martin in the driver's seat, and the three adults joined James and added their weight to the rear of the cart.

Sam, when given the sign by his father, urged the horses on. They needed to be driven quite hard to free the wheels, and even with the pushers doing their part, it took some time to get back onto the hard surface.

In the late afternoon light, another troop were seen in the distance observing them, but little else happened to make the day notable. Camp was again pitched by a small stream. A larger than necessary fire was prepared and lit when it was time to prepare food. They all sat quietly, eating the last of the lamb Sarah had packed for them. Her preserved pickles and boiled cabbage made up the rest of the repast.

The billy had boiled, and tea was passed around. Even the boys, who were usually encouraged to drink other things, were included. Jaiemba had never tasted tea prior to being taken in by the family but had developed a taste for the sweetness of the sugar, which was added generously.

A large log had been dragged into place, and the three adults sat on it, facing the two boys, who were on the far side of the fire on a ground cover. They spoke of the day's events and laughed about how they'd all had to take an early bath to get the wagon back on the road.

Jaiemba suddenly raised his hand, as if to stop the noise. He waited a moment and then stood. Behind the boys, the fire lit up three slowly approaching forms. Martin reached for his gun, but Jaiemba said, 'No.'

He obeyed as the middle figure became visible. It was a very tall Aboriginal man, and his spear was raised. He said a few words. Four more men from his troop appeared from all sides of the camp.

Jaiemba muttered a quiet, controlled challenge, and though the leader raised his spear higher, Jaiemba did not back away even slightly. Seeing his posture and hearing the words he spoke, the spear was lowered a little, and a discourse continued.

Sam explained to his father what he understood. 'They have demanded to know why we are here, and why we have captured Jaiemba. Jaiemba says we are his family, having saved him from being... er, maybe... killed.'

The leader of the troop spoke again, and this time, it was many words before Sam could understand enough to speak. 'I think they're talking about their tribe and where they come from, but I don't know any of the places.'

After a few more tense moments, the leader placed the bottom of his spear on the ground, and all around him followed his action. Some more words came from him, and Jaiemba smiled and nodded.

Sam translated. 'They know... no, they live with Jaiemba's sister.'

Jaiemba neared the leader and bowed his head. The man struck him a light blow on the shoulder with his spear shaft, as if testing his trust, and then Jaiemba said to the family, 'I go.'

There was no great, effusive goodbye, no tears and no physical contact, but the man they had spent time saving looked deep into their eyes, and they all knew his thanks. He shed the European clothing he'd adopted to placate his hosts, and the troop were again swallowed by the fog which surrounded the camp.

Seeing that the boys were feeling somewhat sad Jaiemba was gone, George moved to congratulate them on their action to save another human from an undeserved fate. Though they all agreed this was the best outcome for Jaiemba, both boys were visibly upset.

The group stayed encamped for another night, to make sure that their friend really had gone, and then began the long journey home.

At Bathurst a day later, they stopped and loaded bags of flour, sugar, and other necessities for the farm onto the cart. George never allowed supplies to get low in good times; he knew how hard it could be to locate good produce, let alone pay for it, in times of drought or flood.

George also bought a roll of light blue material he noticed in the window of a larger store. Knowing that Sarah had deliberately deprived herself of a new dress for some time, he decided that it was high time to rectify the situation.

Chapter 5

DURING THE FOLLOWING afternoon, Martin's horse developed a slight limp, and though he could neither see nor feel a reason, Martin took the opportunity to tie his animal to the back of the cart so it wasn't carrying any weight. He mounted the loaded area, moving a few bags to create a comfortable space to take a nap.

'Why, you poor old codger,' George said to him from the driver's seat, though he knew that Martin had driven the cart more than anyone on the trip.

After a short time, Martin felt that he may really go to sleep if he could just get rid of the constant flickering of the sun through the trees and pulled the hessian bags over his head. The boys also wearied at the long trip. Sam swapped with his brother to the middle seat, as he felt he may fall from the side if he dozed off.

Only minutes from the Sofala Road, suddenly, they were confronted by four heavily armed men, two in front and one from either side of the track. All had guns drawn. The two in front held rifles, as did the man on the left. The rider on the right held a pistol, and though the assailants had their faces covered, he spoke in a voice George recognised.

'You will stop,' he demanded.

George had no time to draw a weapon, nor even drive the horses on, as the ambush had been well planned. The narrowing of the track did not allow any leeway.

'What do you want?' George questioned loudly, as the two boys awoke and took a moment to realise what was happening.

'That depends on what contraband you're carrying,' Sheffield's son answered.

'Surely if we were carrying contraband, we would be the ones with covered faces,' George retorted.

'It's not always wise to have a smart word with a gun pointed at your family.'

'Usually, men hiding behind masks are cowards and more mouth than action. Your father will be quick to disown you if you're brought up on charges of highway robbery.'

'Well, let's just see what or who you're carrying before we get into who is breaking the law.'

Sheffield's son quickly mounted the rear of the wagon. Grabbing the edge of the hessian sheet, he pulled it back with the flourish of a magician and was immediately confronted by the double barrels of Martin's shotgun.

This wasn't quite the trick he had planned, and he staggered backwards a few steps with the gun following him.

'There is no doubt who's breaking the law,' Martin said loudly. 'I would be within my rights to shoot you where you stand.'

'You wouldn't dare,' Sheffield said, though his voice didn't sound at all certain.

'Just give me a reason.' Martin was obviously winning the staring competition. 'You other men, put your guns in the back of the wagon and dismount.' He pushed the barrel to encounter the skin of Sheffield's neck.

The three lackeys obeyed. George spurred their mounts to a gallop with his whip, then gave his team a little encouragement, and they trotted on their way home.

Martin gave Sheffield a shove with the gun, and he fell off the back of the cart. Quickly, he regained his feet, swearing. 'You bastard, you can't just leave us here!'

'We just did!' Martin shouted back at them and resumed his position on the rear of the wagon.

'Boy, is that going to cause some trouble,' he murmured as he sat.

'I dare say,' George agreed.

Early the next morning, that trouble rode up to Brucedale in the form of the commander of the local garrison and six of his troopers, along with Sheffield Junior and Senior and the three offsiders from the previous day.

They were met by a closed and barricaded front gate, behind which Martin sat on the wagon's buckboard.

'We thought we might be seeing you today,' he said, tapping his shotgun, which was positioned across his lap.

'Where is Mr Douglas?' the commander demanded.

'I'll just call him for you.' Lifting his gun skywards, Martin fired a shot, which startled several of the horses, and all of Sheffield's men reached for their weapons.

'Calm down, everyone,' the commander ordered. 'Please give warning if you are to fire that again. People may get the wrong idea.'

A few moments passed in the standoff, until George, the two boys and Sarah all came riding up, brandishing rifles.

'What can we do for you, Bracks?' George asked, changing his rifle to the other hand.

Commander Bracks studied him for a moment, then said, 'Hello, George. These men have accused you of ambushing them and taking their weapons.' He paused. 'What do you say to that?'

'Well, I say you've been misled... Young Sheffield here and his cronies ambushed us like highwaymen. They had planned it and came at us from all sides.'

'He's a damned liar,' Sheffield Junior interrupted.

'As I told you at the time, in some places, a man can be hanged for threatening people with loaded guns,' George answered him stoically.

'We were looking for the black they've been harbouring,' one of the other men said. 'And they had *him* in the back with his gun out ready to ambush us.' He pointed to Martin.

'I was asleep under the covers when they came in, shouting and threatening. When this one' – Martin pointed at the younger of the Sheffields – 'boarded the wagon without invitation, he met my gun. He's lucky it didn't go off.'

Bracks considered this for a few seconds and then asked Sheffield Junior, 'Did you mount the wagon without asking?'

'Yes, but we were just trying to–'

'Then it is you who broke the law,' Bracks quickly interrupted him, raising a hand to stop him from speaking.

'Now hold on a moment,' Sheffield Senior interrupted, realising his son had condemned himself. 'There's no need for this bad feeling between neighbours; the boys were just being a bit spirited.'

'That sort of *spirited* gets people killed,' said Bracks.

'You're right, of course. How can we settle this?' Sheffield reached for his money belt.

'We don't want your money. We just want your promise that you'll keep him on a short leash,' George said, motioning toward the now bright red young man.

'You son of a bitch, I'll–'

'Shut up, boy. You've caused enough trouble.' Sheffield scowled at his son. 'I will see that he causes you no more grief.'

'That's good enough,' George said, and nodded to Sheffield.

'You son of a bitch–' the young man started again, almost purple with rage.

'I warned you!' his father shouted. 'Mr Douglas could've had you charged.' He paused for a moment. 'Get out of my sight, and you lot too.'

He turned his gaze on the other three who were involved in the original fracas; they quickly turned their horses and headed off. Sheffield Junior just couldn't leave without a parting word, and as he glared at George, he said, 'You'll pay for this.'

As he turned his horse's head, his father struck it on the rump, and it took to flight, almost losing its rider. The final embarrassment.

'Sorry about all this,' Sheffield said, though it was obvious he too was seething.

'Oh, there were some guns,' Martin said and produced a hessian bag full of gun parts, 'I gave them a good, ah... clean.'

Sheffield took the bag and gave a rueful smile; he blushed almost as much as his son did. He turned his horse and rode off without looking back.

'Sorry about this, Douglas,' Bracks said. 'He's a dangerous man when riled up. I wouldn't let my guard down if I were you.' Then he nodded, and he and his men cantered away.

The incident affected the way the family conducted their day-to-day lives. George insisted that the boys not go out alone and, when riding the boundary fences, that they do so in pairs. Trips into the town were usually a whole-family affair, though if Sarah insisted on remaining at home, the two boys stayed with her. This was a much more defensive way of living; it took some getting used to. George and Martin took no chances and impressed upon Sarah and the boys that the Sheffield family had little or no compunction in mistreating others.

Sarah, over the next day or two, fell ill again with influenza. The midwife was called for, and though she applied all the recommended treatments, the baby was stillborn.

So devastating to Sarah was the loss that she stayed in her room for several days, avoiding contact with all the world, all except George. Her interaction with him for the first two days was limited to nods. She didn't want him to see how helpless and distraught she felt.

Eventually, one morning, the sound and smell of breakfast came from the kitchen. As the boys entered and kissed their mother's face, their usual morning greeting, each knew to say nothing more unless the subject was raised by Sarah herself.

The topic was never mentioned again between the men of the house and Sarah. This was for women to understand, and the discussions came with other women when the wound became less painful.

Chapter 6

ALMOST TWELVE MONTHS passed, and the weather again reverted to drought. The land was a dust bowl. Stock were starving in the paddocks.

George and Martin had prepared well for this eventuality and filled twenty-three large wine barrels with water for household use and another for use in the barn. They knew this did not drought-proof the farm by any means, but the extra few weeks may be just enough to get them through.

The farm was on undulating land. Two thirds of the paddocks were on higher ground, and the dams in each were already emptied. All of the stock had been moved to the front five paddocks, as there was still some water in their dams, and in the second-closest to the homestead, there was a small wetland fed year-round by a natural spring. This spring would also run dry if the rains didn't come, but it gave George a little more time to prepare to sell stock if it was necessary.

The dryness of the winter surprised them, and when the bitter winds came in August, George decided that the time had come to look for a possible buyer of the lesser cattle; this would allow him to keep his breeding stock and the two milking cows. Consequentially, George, Martin and the two boys travelled to the Bathurst cattle markets to take a good look at the situation in which all owners found themselves.

Arriving at the sale yards, they were all shocked by the scene which greeted them. Owners were clamouring over the tall wooden fences to grab at the cattle, pushing and pulling at the beasts to see exactly what flesh and muscle tone was left, if any.

'This could be pretty rough, George,' said Martin, and George nodded his agreement.

George led the boys past the auctioneer and mounted a pen fence three ahead of the one being auctioned. 'These are the kind of cattle I'm interested in; see how they have a grey colour?'

'They're awfully poor and thin?' said James questioningly.

'Yes indeed. That's why we should be able to get at least a couple of breeding cows for our bull.'

'So, you're breeding a whole new breed, then?' Sam asked.

'Well, I wouldn't exactly say that,' George explained, as the auction moved another pen closer. 'I want to breed some of the traits from the greys into our herd. They have bigger hindquarters and seem to be more resistant to lack of water.'

He paused. 'We didn't come to buy, but we may not get a better chance.' He turned to Martin, and Martin nodded his agreement.

George knew that James was interested in the farming of cattle, while Sam showed no interest at all; still, he offered them both the same information. The auction moved to the yard next to them. The calling of the auctioneer sounded quite strange to both boys, and they looked at their father for information.

'Auctioneers all speak fast like that. Not sure why; perhaps it's to stir the buyers up,' he said, and the auctioneer moved to their stall.

Quickly, he began to babble in terms which only allowed the boys to understand a word here and there. They saw their father raise his hand and say, 'Two,' and in the end, he said, 'For three.' There were no other bids.

So, having bought three breeding cows, George moved to pay for them. He knew that would put a stress on the farm's financial situation but would, in the long term, pay off.

Martin directed the boys to go and get the four horses and meet back at the pen, where they would pick out the three cows and drove them home. As they obeyed and turned into the short street where they'd left their horses tied to a rail, they found themselves confronted by Sheffield Junior and his three thugs.

'Look what we have here, boys. A couple of nigger lovers,' the vile young man said, and his cohort laughed. He stepped up to James and gave him a push in the chest, which almost knocked him over. Though Sheffield was a good foot taller than James, and perhaps five or six years older, James flew back at him with clenched fists, striking an uppercut which also almost toppled him.

Immediately, fists flew wildly. Though both boys had been taught to protect themselves by Martin, their size, and the fact that they were outnumbered two to one, soon saw the gang getting the upper hand. Sam was still hampered by his injured leg, but he gave as good as he got before being caught by one of the thugs from behind and struck several hard blows by another, which felled him.

James was similarly caught, but as Sheffield came near to deal the same cowardly blows, James lifted both his feet off the ground, using the man behind him as support, and landed a kick in the middle of Sheffield's chest. This knocked him off his feet. As he drew his knife and began to get up, he heard the click of a rifle being cocked at the side of his head.

He froze and looked at the long barrel which confronted him. Behind it was a woman. 'I don't think you'll be wanting to use that knife,' she said calmly. 'Go on, get home to your father.' She pushed the barrel even closer to his face.

Sheffield backed off, still on the ground, saying, 'You'll pay for this, bitch,' as he regained his feet.

'I don't think so, boy. It was your father who told me not to let you get into any trouble at my establishment. Now get home and give him my regards.' She waved the barrel at Sheffield and then his offsiders. Expletives burst from his lips in an incoherent babble before two of his friends dragged him away.

Sam was still on the ground, holding his jaw, and James moved to help him up, saying, 'Thank you, ma'am.'

The woman, who must have been in her late forties or early fifties, was dressed to look much younger, unsuccessfully. 'That's alright, young man. I saw what happened from inside. He's a mean-spirited cur, that one.' She motioned toward a building, and the boys followed with their eyes.

Very quickly, they both realised it was the local bordello. 'Madam Sophie Proprietor', as the garish sign proclaimed, had saved them.

The boys were both surprised, and neither could find any more words. Seeing their embarrassment, Sophie decided to have a little fun.

'You boys are a little too young to be darkening my doorstep,' she said.

The boys looked at each other, not knowing what to say.

'Well, cat got your tongue?' she pushed, almost laughing.

'No, we wouldn't – ah, that is, we weren't, um,' babbled Sam.

'Oh, we aren't good enough for you, then?' she snarled at him.

'Um no, he didn't mean any insult, ma'am,' James spluttered.

Sophie laughed uproariously, and said, 'It's alright, boys, but you better be on your way, and tell your Uncle Martin he owes me big time.'

Both boys smiled, realising she'd been having a joke at their expense. They dusted themselves off, untied the horses, and began to ride back to the saleyards. Sophie stood at the door of her establishment, and as they passed, she said, 'You all come back when you're old enough.'

Both boys blushed bright red but did not answer as they trotted away.

On reaching the yards, Martin said, 'Where the heck have you two been?'

Receiving no immediate answer, he took a better look at them. Sam still had a bloody nose, and James was developing a black eye and missing his hat.

'What happened?' Martin demanded, as their father strode up.

The boys looked at each other, and James answered, 'It was Sheffield and his gang.'

'They started a fight, and James sat Sheffield on his butt, then Sheffield came back with a knife, and that's when Madam Sophie stopped him with a big gun,' blurted Sam, running all the words together in his excitement.

'What were you doing at Madam Sophie's?' questioned Martin with tongue in cheek.

'We weren't. She came out when she saw the trouble, and she said you owe her big time,' Sam said.

'The things I have to do for you Douglases,' Martin complained and shook his head.

The boys blushed and smiled. No more was said about the matter on the way back to Brucedale.

Chapter 7

CLANDESTINE HARASSMENT CONTINUED over the next few months, with fences cut and gates deliberately left open. The area again transitioned into drought. The family, who had sold most of their lower-grade stock the previous year, now needed to protect their remaining animals very carefully if they wished to save the breeding herd.

George had all of the cattle brought into the two forwardmost paddocks, where the spring still filled the waterholes. He also hired two workhands, a middle-aged man and young boy. The man was known as Carter, and the eleven-year-old Leo.

These were not the most brilliant choices to fill the position, one being a bit past his prime and the other very green, but they had arrived at the homestead one day having come penniless from Bathurst in the west. Sarah had fed them, and George decided to offer them bed and board for their assistance with the cattle and sheep. Carter jumped at the chance and almost single-handedly doubled the amount of food Sarah had to prepare each day.

Leo proved to be a favourite with Sarah, as he was quite an artist, creating the most beautiful leatherwork, repairing shoes and even making small wood carvings. Indeed, a kangaroo he had created stood realistically looking across the room from the mantle above the fire in Sarah's kitchen. It seemed that whenever the boy was not working with the animals, he was creating something.

This was the second year in succession where the late winter and early spring rains had not come. This year, by design, there were less cattle to move. Only the best of the new breed and a few older cows were left. The old bull, though he showed his displeasure, was placed in a holding pen behind the house and hand-fed grain.

George decided that he and Martin would have to travel to Bathurst and access some water from the river to fulfil the needs of the household. The river still flowed, though it too was much diminished in capacity. The wagon was loaded with casks, which George had acquired with the intention of trying to make wine in the future. Carter accompanied them with three buckets, which were the only way they had to fill said casks.

The four horses had been hitched to pull the heavy load back, and Martin had also taken his own mount. Little more than an hour after they had left, the three boys, who were engaged in cleaning the barn and mucking out the stables, heard a stifled scream from the direction of the house.

Sarah had been startled by the sudden appearance behind her in the vegetable garden of three very dubious-looking men.

'What do you want?' she shouted, hoping the boys would hear and take cover.

'Dangerous place for a lady to be left alone,' one of the assailants said threateningly.

'What do you want?' demanded Sarah again, trying not to look scared. She edged toward the house, but one of the men moved to intercept her. As he grabbed at her, a shot tore his shoulder apart. Sam's aim was as true, as usual, and the man fell as if dead.

In the several seconds it took the other men to retrieve their rifles, Sarah had entered the rear of the house and slammed and bolted the back door. She was immediately met by Sam and Leo, who handed her the rifle she kept in the kitchen behind the pantry door.

As the two other men advanced toward the house, they were met by covering fire from James, who lay on the roof in a protected spot Martin had created for just this kind of situation.

'Close all the shutters,' ordered Sarah, running from one room to the next to make sure the doors and windows were secured. James came down through a shutter in the roof and locked it behind him.

Sam assumed the front-of-house position, along with Leo. They had practiced this with George and Martin, and there were spy-holes at both ends of the front wall. These allowed two shooters to cover the area from the front fences to the sheds, which were to the left of the house. James and his mother went to similar positions at the rear of the building, and very quickly, they'd covered most of the areas around the house.

'What do you think they want?' Sam shouted.

'Everything,' Sarah replied, as she noticed one of the men dart from an external building to the water stand. The man who'd been felled in the garden made his way to one of the feeding troughs and quickly hid behind it.

'Do we shoot to kill?' asked Leo in a trembling, frightened voice.

'Yes,' answered Sarah. 'There is no other way.'

Sam looked across at Leo and saw that he was shaking. It was obvious he'd never been in a position where real bullets were used to kill. Likewise, Sam had not been in a similar situation either.

'You slow them down, and I'll do the rest,' Sam reassured him, and though Leo was scared, he nodded.

For a short time, nothing happened. Then four other horsemen were seen entering the front gate. They were out of firing range and rapidly took cover behind the main barn.

Now there were six able-bodied men and a wounded one surrounding the house. Sarah looked stoic, but James could see a tear on her cheek.

'We could hold on here for weeks. We have plenty of food and water,' he said reassuringly.

'I know, but I worry for your father and Martin,' she answered, and James saw another tear glisten and run down her face.

One of the aggressors showed his head around the right corner of the shed and was immediately met by a shot from Leo's gun. He didn't hit the man but rather the small water tank at the rear side of the tack yard. This so startled the man that his hat fell off, and it sat for a time in full view in front of the shed. As his hand slowly moved to recover it, another shot rang out, this time from Sam's gun. It passed through the shed wall and obviously hit the man, who fell into view and was dragged away by his friends.

'Great shot,' said Leo excitedly, though it was not a joyous excitement.

'It may calm them down for a while,' said Sam, as another shot rang out from behind the house.

'What do you think they want?' asked Leo again, with a quaver in his voice.

'They'll be failed gold miners or bush rangers or horse rustlers,' said James. 'Whatever they are, they mean business.'

Suddenly, there was the smell of smoke.

'They've set the barn on fire,' Sam blurted.

The two horses had been let out and ran quickly toward the front dam. One of the men used them to gain cover behind the larger of two disused water tanks, but as he arrived, Leo's gun fired, and he fell dead. Leo was shocked. The gun fell from his hands.

Seeing his face, Sam said, 'It's us or them.'

Though Leo knew this was true, his realisation that he'd killed a living being weighed heavily on him, and he wept.

Piercing the glass of the rear window, five or six shots cracked into the shutters. One smashed through and blew a hole in the large honey pot on the mantelpiece. This was covering fire for one of the men to get to his wounded companion behind the water trough. He was carrying two rifles and made his cover despite the shots of Sarah and James.

Now the rear of the house was more unsafe than the front. The two rifles behind the trough fired together, and a third man ran to the rear of the outhouse at the left side of the yard, reaching his ground safely. This created a crossfire and made it much more difficult for James and Sarah to defend their positions. Sarah, however, waited and waited for the man to show himself for just a moment from behind the toilet, and when he dared to raise his gun and prepare to shoot, she took her chance and he also fell dead.

Sarah too had misgivings about taking a life, but she would do anything to protect her children.

Soon after, a shot from the water tank smashed through the wall where James stood and entered his thigh just inches below his hip. He dropped to the floor, though he hardly issued a sound. Sarah saw him fall and said quickly, 'Are you alright?'

She couldn't tell that he'd been hit, and as he sprung up swiftly, she didn't know how dangerous the wound was.

In front of the house, there were huge billows of black smoke from the barn and visibility was almost nil. Sam knew that the charge would come at the door, and Leo was crouched there, so he shouted, 'Swap places!'

Leo obeyed, and they each gained the other's spot safely.

Something smashed against the front wall. The door and wall next to it burst into flames. Sam looked around the room and suddenly jumped up, running to the large dining table and turning it over so there was cover behind it. He pulled it to the doorway between the two front rooms and, diving behind it, called Leo to join him.

The younger boy hurled himself over the table. Though there were several shots, none hit him. He'd gained safety – at least till the next onslaught.

Sarah, seeing this new line of defence, could predict the attack would soon come from the front. She joined the two boys behind the table, leaving James to protect the rear and trusting he would call for help if he needed it.

They were all aware they were in dire straits if the fire got into the roof.

Suddenly, they heard more horses galloping in through the front gate and shots being fired. Their hearts fell, as now there was little chance that they could hold on. For a few moments, the firing became frantic, but Sarah realised that no bullets were coming through the building.

'It's help! They have the two at the back at gunpoint!' James shouted.

Soon, the shooting stopped. Several horses could be heard madly galloping away, and several shots were fired after them.

'Hello in the house!' a deep voice shouted.

There was a pause, as the four inside didn't know what was happening.

'Hello, Douglases,' the voice boomed again.

'Hello?' answered Sarah in a questioning tone.

'Buckets, hurry,' Sheffield ordered his men. 'Here... We'll try to put the fire out.'

Within a few minutes, water could be heard dousing the fire, first near the front door and then along the whole front of the building. The house had been well made, and the door was of the heaviest hardwood. It would've taken hours to burn out.

As soon as the fire was extinguished, Sarah opened the door and exited, followed by Sam and Leo.

'We saw the smoke from the main road. Are you all alright?' questioned Sheffield, who sat on his beautiful black steed, having directed the rescue from this vantage point.

Sarah and the boys looked round. 'I think so. Where's James?' questioned Sam.

He rushed back inside to find his brother on the floor in a pool of blood. He had obviously passed out. Sam screamed for help.

Sarah dashed to his side and immediately called for bandages to stop the bleeding. Sheffield had dismounted and helped to lift James onto the kitchen table.

'Able, in here,' he shouted, and soon, the summoned man entered. 'This is Jake Able, Mrs Douglas. We call him Doc. He's the best for this kind of thing.' He pointed at the wound.

Sarah wasn't keen on owing anything to Sheffield, but James's life was more important than any petty dislike. She nodded her consent, and the 'Doc' came to the table and looked at his patient.

'Hot water and my kit,' he muttered, placing his hand over the wound, which still oozed blood at a fair rate. Sam had returned with the bandages, and Able took one, made a tourniquet and quickly secured it above the wound. This was difficult, as the bullet had entered high on the thigh.

Able cut away the leg of the trousers with Sarah's carving knife to get at the wound properly. With the arrival of his tools of trade, he immediately found and removed the bullet. At this point, James came around and yelled loudly, not sure what was happening.

Reassured on one side by his mother and the other by Sam, he never let out another yell while the diligent Doc removed several large wooden splinters and many small ones. He washed the wound with the hottest water he thought the boy could stand, and then continued the slow and gruelling task of removing the remaining small splinters one by one.

When clean, the wound was stitched. Sarah had treated many injuries, but knew the job done by the Doc was far more professional than anything she could've managed.

'Thank you,' she said, and then faltered for the first time herself.

She would have fallen if Sheffield hadn't been right next to her. He helped her to a nearby chair, and Sam came to her side.

'Thank you, sir,' he said and put his hand forward to shake the older man's. Sheffield met it with a strong grip and, with his other hand, patted Sam on the shoulder.

'You have done your mother proud today, boy.' He turned to Leo. 'You too, young man.'

Leo nodded, always being short of words when with an important elder.

'We'll make sure everything in the yard is safe and wait until your husband gets home,' Sheffield said. 'I think that lot of scum will be as far away from here as they can get, but it's better to be safe than sorry.'

'Thank you so much,' said Sarah. 'I'll make some food and send it out with the boys.' She stood and headed to the stove.

In the midafternoon, George and Martin rode back into the property, not for a moment expecting to be met with the carnage of the morning. Immediately as they entered through the open gate, they could see some horses they knew did not belong. A body was draped over the nearest of the steeds.

George increased his speed and now could see the front of the house, burned but still standing, with a small plume of smoke emitting from one corner. Rushing past the group of men who sat in a circle consuming tea and scones, he leapt from his horse and ran to the remnants of the front door.

As he burst in, Sam and Leo jumped from their seats and came to him. He hugged them but waited for no explanations, rushing to the kitchen to look for Sarah.

They embraced, and he kissed her forehead as she imparted the story of what had happened. Martin had also entered and heard the details as he hugged the two boys. He let Leo know that Carter had decided to stay in town overnight, as not all the items they'd gone to town for were available.

George and Martin were both surprised to hear that it was Sheffield's men, and indeed Sheffield himself, who had come to the rescue. They poured out of the house to thank the men individually and Sheffield in particular.

'I thank you for my family,' said George, as he shook the other's hand and then pulled him close and hugged him.

Sheffield was overcome, and re-making his personal space, said, 'It's what we all must do when someone is in trouble.'

Martin moved to Sheffield next and gripped his hand. 'Perhaps we all got off to a bad start, but there is nothing braver you could've done than save our family.'

'My pleasure.' Sheffield mounted his horse, which one of the men had brought for him from behind the shed. 'We'll take this one,' he said, motioning toward the body on the last horse. 'Someone will know who he is, and we may be able to find out who the others were.'

'Thank you again,' said Sarah, and all the family added to her comment.

As Sheffield passed the far end of the house, he turned his horse and said, 'Should I leave a couple of men for the night, just in case?'

'No, thank you. You've done more than enough,' George answered.

The party rode slowly away. Sarah waved several times, though the riders never looked back.

The next day, on Carter's return, they all heard about the 'great battle at the Douglas place'. The story had reached town and grown to massive proportions. Three boys and one woman fighting off thirty bushrangers for a day, until they were saved by Sheffield and his men, was one such rumour. They all laughed when they heard the tall tale, knowing that thirty men would've taken the place in a few minutes.

The laughter soon died down when they heard that the next farm to the north had been raided before their own, and that Parson Wilson had been killed and 'Old Lady Wilson' wounded after blowing one of the bushrangers away with a double-barrelled shotgun. These were people with little money or possessions to their name, but what they had, the bandits readily took, before setting fire to the house. Carter could not tell Sarah, who immediately asked, how the old lady was, but she had been taken to the midwife's cottage for care.

The next morning, Martin and George, accompanied by Sam and Leo, loaded tools onto the cart and moved to one of the farm's back acres to cut logs for repairing the house. James was peeved at being left out because of his wounded leg but took up position on the front veranda with said leg up, a rifle in one hand and a cold drink in the other. Carter and Sarah filled a huge black caldron with hard tar, lit a fire in the front yard and started to rend the tar to repair the damaged roof.

Over the next three days, the house was abuzz as all the farms around sent every able-bodied person to help with the repairs. In the end, there were more people than jobs, and George began by welcoming newcomers and then trying to send them home again. No one took the slightest bit of notice, and on the third day, a great feast of two full lambs and a hindquarter of beef was cooked on spits in the garden for the thirty-five men and twenty women who were on site.

The women sat on chairs and barrels with a plank of wood stretched between to create more seating at the rear of the house. The men sat nearer to the big barn on stumps, buckets and anything else which might be converted to a seat.

This became a kind of community event which George remembered from England. The major difference was that in England, it only seemed to happen when someone had died.

James was paraded around the ring of men for handshakes and pats on the back, while in the women's circle, it was kisses and 'Oh, you poor little man.' Sam and Leo had forced him into the limelight and delighted even more at his discomfort when the women began to talk of what a fine husband he was going to make and who were likely brides in the district. Sam only let him escape when talk turned to his 'dear little brother' also becoming a groom.

After most of the food was eaten, when people were beginning to move off to work again, George stood on a chair and called everyone to order.

'This is the most wonderful community spirit,' he started and faltered a little as everyone gave a cheer or clapped as the mood took them. 'We must build on this; we must make a true community of our district. It's so wonderful to see people here from nearly every farm from as far and wide as I can imagine. The future for us all... There will be more hard times, more destruction, more moments when we need friends to count on. Great friends like I see when I look around me today.'

There was a great outburst of delight from everyone.

'You have lightened our hearts, so please, eat your fill, and have an afternoon to remember,' he concluded, to cheers from all assembled.

One man stepped forward and shook George's hand, saying, 'That sounded like an election speech. You should stand for mayor.'

George laughed, but the people around him knew him to be a leader among men, someone they could trust.

Chapter 8

MERLE WILSON, AFTER recovering from her wounds, was added to the Douglas family as cook and cleaner. Sarah and George had offered her the position knowing she had no chance of staying in the old farmhouse now that the pastor was dead. They were really just making a place for her, as it was obvious Sarah had no need for help. The extra body did come in handy, though, as Sarah announced that she was again pregnant, and the beautiful, red-headed Gertrude was born.

Just a few short days later, Mrs Wilson, who'd been invaluable at the birth, caught influenza and passed away in less than forty-eight hours. Her health had never been particularly good after the loss of her husband, and the speed with which she had been taken surprised no one. The old woman was laid to rest in the Douglas family graveyard. Soon after, Gertie contracted a fever and also passed quickly. The family were distraught as they laid her to rest in the same graveyard within a week.

Sarah returned to work two days after her daughter's funeral. She spoke to no one and showed as little emotion as possible. She too weakened and contracted a fever, though she was spared after a week's convalescence. She fought her way back to health, saying that there was work to be done. There was, in reality, little to do, as the area moved into yet another year of drought.

George had purchased the Wilson property the previous year and now found himself stretched. It was impossible to begin fencing repairs on the long-neglected paddocks, and in October, he put the extra land up for sale.

Soon they were neighbours to the great landowners Sheffield and son. For almost six months, this made little or no difference to daily life. They were fighting the land for a living, a living that the land did not give easily.

This drought was even more biting than the previous two. Not only was there no real rain to speak of, but there were weeks of very high temperatures and strong winds. Then started three weeks of dust storms, which scoured the land and tore away the topsoil. Still, the Douglas property's front three paddocks, those closest to the east fence line, were relatively protected, sloping away as they did from the west.

In the middle of February, the Aboriginal troop who had helped Sam suddenly appeared at the front dam, and though there were as many as a dozen very young children, it was obvious that all were in a debilitated state. As always, when the rains didn't come, game was harder to find, and the children's distended bellies were more than enough to show how long they had been affected.

Going to the storeroom, Sarah took a bucket of apples and gave them to Sam. She also gathered the last of the damper, which she always kept in a bread safe, handing it to Leo. No sooner had he, James and Sam left the building than more damper was being made, and whole potatoes were in pans being cooked.

All three boys approached the mob, slowly repeating greetings. They were met by two of the stronger-looking men and challenged. Sam offered the apples, holding them high in front of him, and Leo copied him with the damper.

The men looked at the offerings suspiciously and restrained one of the younger children who came to take food. Seeing their reluctance, Sam took a piece of the damper and bit into it, then did the same with an apple. He placed both containers on the ground and stood well back.

The elder women took the offerings and divided them among the troop, after one of the elder men tasted everything, looking to the youngest and most feeble first. Sam said a few words he remembered, which he thought meant 'more' and that he would come back, and the three boys returned to the house.

Sarah was hard at work, and the smell of cooking pervaded the house and beyond. To Sarah, these were her neighbours as much as any others, and they needed help.

The boys spent a considerable amount of time ferrying the food to the camp and being greeted ever more enthusiastically. Sarah had included many different dishes and pastries, including her jam biscuits; however, the taster, who still checked everything, quickly rejected these. Though James ate one, the taster waved the leftovers away. Perhaps the jam was too sweet for their palate. Returning to let Sarah know that they had been rejected, the boys were handed another three loaves of damper, and they left the biscuits as directed.

After about three hours, George, Martin and Carter arrived home and were surprised to see the banquet on their front doorstep. As they entered the house, it was obvious there was no danger and that the feast had been provided at will.

Sarah still had plenty of food prepared for the men and the boys, so they all sat and enjoyed the meal together. They discussed the way the visitors arrived, and how thirsty and hungry they were. George knew that Sarah would never turn anyone away who was starving, and he thanked her. He remembered the days of hunger in England, sitting waiting for soup made of little more than salt, water and a soup bone boiled for the third or fourth time. He would also never see anyone go hungry, even if it meant the loss of his last penny.

After eating, the whole family walked down to greet the visitors. The men were met somewhat nervously at first, but soon all were talking as if they were long-lost friends. From what Martin could understand, they were chased off the land to the southeast the day before by a group of horsemen, led by a 'young evil one' who shot at them when they tried to go through a fence. The man wouldn't let them use his waterhole.

'Probably Sheffield Junior,' Martin mused, and George nodded. 'He'll cause no end of trouble if he finds out they're here.'

George continued to nod then shrugged his shoulders. 'Can't see that we can do a lot about it,' he said. Martin shook his head.

After a few minutes thinking, George said, 'We could move them up the back twenty. One of the seven dams has a little water and a bit of a spring.'

'Let's see what the morning brings. The troop will probably move off anyway,' answered Martin, and they both nodded as Martin took a large puff of his cigarette.

The three boys were approached by the only teenage youth in the troop. Soon, they found themselves involved in a game which included all the camp's children. It appeared to the adults to be a kind of tug-of-war, though there was no rope. At one stage, Leo was the only one still standing and was immediately heralded as the winner. He wasn't even sure what he'd done but took the applause with great delight.

Though it was long since dark, and times weren't exactly at their best for travelling after the sun receded, Carter arrived with a laden cart, and all who lived at the farm moved off to help him unpack.

Immediately, Carter saw a chance. He called George aside and let him know that he'd seen a large party of men camping near the creek, headed by Sheffield Junior.

'They were full of grog, and I reckon they were looking for as much trouble as they could get into.'

George said nothing for a few moments, so the older man pushed the point. 'They wouldn't take well to the visitors in your front yard.'

'No, I guess not,' George said and thought for a while again. 'Finish unpacking the wagon and then come inside.'

Carter nodded and went back to work; George took a small box meant for the kitchen and headed inside.

In just a few minutes, the goods to be stored in the barn were under lock and key, and the two boys had fed and brushed the horses which pulled the wagon. They entered the kitchen to see the adults all sitting at the table. A plate of food had been prepared for Carter by Sarah, and he ate with the fervour of a lead working dog.

George signalled for everyone to sit down and was quickly and quietly obeyed.

'There are a group of low-lifes camping down by the river just after the crossroads,' George started. 'Carter saw them from the road. They're doing a lot of drinking and are, no doubt, out for trouble.' He paused for a moment. 'Our visitors will need to move early in the morning. I'm going to lead them up the back paddock. We'll need to get all the women and elders on the cart and move as early as we can.'

Everyone nodded. As was to be expected, George's word was law.

'Boys, you'll need to come with me to explain what we have to do.'

Sam and James followed him, and on the walk down the hill,

George asked if they thought they could make the elders understand the plight they were in, if the boys had enough of the language.

'Sam can speak fairly fluently,' answered James.

'I think I can do it, but I'm not sure they'll take me seriously, not being an adult,' Sam said.

'Well, we just have to make it work,' their father added.

As they approached, one of the stronger-looking men challenged them. It was hard to see more than the three figures approaching in the light of the dwindling campfire. Sam said a few words, and they were led to the elders, who were positioned with their backs to the fence line.

Sam gestured toward George, saying that he was speaking for his father. To his surprise, the elders gave him their full attention. He had bothered to learn as much of their language as he could, and they respected the effort.

Soon, the agreement was made, though several of the younger men stood and displayed their spears to show how they would protect against all comers. The elders, however, knew too well how devastating the white man's weapons could be.

Carter and Leo carried out the hitching of the wagon and saddling of the horses. It had been decided that they would stay with Sarah in case they had unwelcome visitors.

As the last of the women and children were loaded on the wagon in the breaking light, a sole horseman moved past the entrance to the farm and then turned and cantered off in the direction from which he'd come. Martin saw the man and neared George, asking if he'd also noticed.

'Yes, I suppose that means we'll have company,' George replied. 'Make sure everyone has their guns handy.'

The group moved off as quickly as the two elder men could walk. They had refused to ride on the cart, but after a couple of miles, they were convinced that it was for the good of the whole troop if they mounted.

Sam, who had been riding alongside his father, got down and helped one of the men onto the wagon's front seat. The other got onto the back with the women. Sam then mounted James's horse with his brother. As they would be trotting at best, James's horse would be more than able to carry them both.

They travelled for more than two hours across tracks which at times seemed to disappear entirely into the surrounding paddocks. The white trunks of the eucalypts in front of them glowed pink as the morning offered forth a beautiful spectacle of reds and yellows in the few clouds which dotted the horizon. The sun rose at their backs, but that was not what they all kept looking over their shoulders to see. Though they were on their own land, they felt sure that Sheffield Junior and his band of louts wouldn't take much notice of fences if they intended to carry out some act of bastardry.

They reached the final watering hole, and no sign of the ruffians had been seen. Martin and George spoke for a few minutes as the passengers disembarked, and Sam dismounted his brother's horse and resumed his position next to his father. Quickly, they bade the troop farewell and turned back. All were thinking that if the Sheffield posse hadn't chased them, perhaps they were causing trouble at the farm. They barely looked over their shoulders, other than to wave a fleeting goodbye.

On arrival back at the farmhouse, they were met by Sarah, Carter and Leo, who assured them that nobody had passed their way and that it had been quiet all day. The horses were unhitched and led into the barn by Carter. He and Leo had prepared food for the horses but let them drink their fill first at the troughs. Likewise, Sarah had prepared hot food for the four.

While washing up in the human trough alongside the horses', George and Martin discussed the day and what should be expected of Sheffield Junior and his cohort.

'What do you think they'll do?' asked Martin.

George didn't have a ready answer. He shrugged, and then, after a minute thinking, he said, 'I think we should go out there again tomorrow.'

Martin nodded.

Chapter 9

DUE TO A heavy frost overnight, the grass gleamed white, and the sun's rays searched for patches to melt. George and Martin saddled their horses as quietly as they could. They intended to slip away and not disturb the rest of the household. Sam and James, however, were aware of every move they'd made and were up and dressed, ready to go with them. James appeared next to his father, and Sam led his and his brother's horses into the stall to be saddled.

'You boys should stay here; we don't know if there will be trouble or not,' George said, though he didn't for a moment think they were going to take no for an answer.

'You need to let us come,' answered James.

'Don't you tell me what I need to do,' scolded his father. While he did want the boys to stay home, he didn't sound as strong as he might have.

'Sorry, but you may need to speak to the elders, and only Sam can do that,' James answered.

'It could be dangerous–' George started but was cut off mid-stream by Sam.

'We are coming!' he exclaimed, as he threw a saddle over the back of the second horse.

George looked to Martin for an opinion, and Martin nodded. Nothing more was said as the four rode out of the yard and headed for the camp.

On reaching the waterhole, there was no trace of the troop. They had moved, and even with the masterful tracking skills which Martin possessed, he could find no way to follow them.

'We'll check along the back fence line,' George said, and they moved off at a canter.

They rode along the western and southern fences and eventually came back to the east fence and the track, which led them home. They saw no sign of the mob.

They returned home, feeling secure that if they couldn't track the mob, a bunch of drunk louts would have little chance.

Though the drought became much worse, the front dam of the Douglas farm stayed fairly full. Fed by the permanent spring, the water was being drained. The household tanks had long since run out, and barrelled water was being used. The farmyard animals, particularly the geese and ducks, along with the horses when stabled, needed to drink regularly, and it seemed that each day started with filling and loading barrels onto the cart to bring water to the house. The three boys mostly did this, though sometimes, Carter would be up and start with Leo before anyone else stirred.

Very few trips into Bathurst occurred during these months, as there was little money to spend, and 'making do' was the name of the game. The storehouse was still about half full of grain, and there was a glut of beef. They had to kill many of their breeding stock, as there simply wasn't enough flow from the spring to keep them alive. A minimum of thirty cows and their breeding bull were being watered in the next paddock, for they would've trampled the sides of the dam if they were allowed to use it directly. It was difficult enough for the boys to keep mud out of the barrels, and a distinct taste of the earth became accepted. Sarah boiled water for about twenty hours a day to drink, but even in the tea, the taste of the land was evident. No one complained; that was just how it was, and complaining would help no one.

As December approached, there was no relief. No rain of any substance had fallen in the area for nearly twelve months, and the bitter drought scorched the land near and far. Even the front dam at

Brucedale had run dry. Sarah had filled as many containers of boiled water as she could, and the kitchen had barely a flat space which wasn't covered. Even the large mixing bowl was full of water and sat in the sink. Likewise, the barn was full of barrelled water left to settle.

Everyone suffered in these long dry spells. Some prepared well, and it was expected that the richest man in the area would've been better prepared than most. However, early one morning, Sheffield rode up to the farm and dismounted. George and Sarah, seated on the front porch, greeted him and were as pleasant as they could be with a man who neither could bring themselves to like.

'Morning,' he said and tied his horse to the hitching rail.

'Morning,' they both answered.

'Damned dry,' he added. 'Oh, sorry, Mrs Douglas. I don't get to speak to many ladies these days.'

'That's quite alright. How can we help you, Mr Sheffield?' Sarah answered.

'Well, I won't beat around the bush. I'm not used to asking for help, but the creek has stopped running, and though I had large waterholes dug along its course, well, um, it has gone stagnant, green as grass.' He stumbled over these words and then, after a pause, added, 'I have no water at all and wondered if you would sell me some?'

'We'll help you as much as we can,' stated George, 'but we have no stock water available. I think we could spare a couple of barrels of house water.'

'I understand. It's only good business to hold out for the best price,' Sheffield remarked.

'You misunderstand,' George said. 'We'll give you the house water, but now it's down to the water we have stored. Our spring's dry also.'

'None of your dams are carrying?' Sheffield asked in desperation.

'Nothing other than a bit of damp mud,' George returned.

'It'll ruin us all.' Sheffield removed his hat and looked at the sky.

'The rains will come again soon,' Sarah said, trying to lift his spirits.

'I don't think they will in time. I have seven hundred head just dying in the paddocks.'

'I'm sorry we can't help more,' she answered.

'No, no, it's my own fault. The creek has only stopped flowing once before, and the waterholes were still pretty full when the rains came that time.' As he remounted his horse, Sheffield said, 'I'll send someone over this afternoon to collect the two barrels. Thank you for your kindness.' He turned his horse and rode off.

'He stands to lose his fortune,' Sarah said as he passed the gate.

'Men like him never lose their fortune. You watch; he'll be buying up other properties as they fall,' George said.

'You just don't like him,' Sarah said, and as George lifted his eyebrows, she added, 'Neither do I.'

The three boys and Carter had been out on the wagon picking up the weakest cattle and placing the dead onto piles. The piles weren't very high at this stage but would grow before being burned.

In the late afternoon, Sheffield Junior and two other men arrived on what looked like a brand-new buckboard. Martin, who had just returned from points unknown, took them to the barn and helped them load the two barrels. Sheffield made a surly comment about the amount of water they had left, saying that his father should have all of it, as he was going to own the entire valley one day anyhow.

'Over my dead body,' Martin said, not frightened to stare the young man down, even if he had two offsiders.

'That could be arranged,' Sheffield snarled.

'Only by backstabbing dogs,' Martin said, smiling.

The three men remounted the wagon and Sheffield, who was used to having the last word, said, 'Don't be too sure of yourself.' He grabbed the reins.

'I'm right here, waiting,' Martin concluded.

George joined him. 'Is there a problem?' he asked, as the angry young man slapped the horses.

On returning to the house, Martin and George found the rest of the family seated at the dinner table waiting for them.

'That boy is going to be trouble,' Martin said, washing his hands in a metal bowl of soapy water. George didn't reply but followed him in washing, and they sat down to the meal.

James said grace. The food was fine, with both beef and lamb, and heaped mashed potatoes. There were only a few green peas in a bowl, as the gardens were almost done. Everyone avoided the peas and the small, sliced tomato, except Leo, who dug in and took half of the tomato in one scoop. He hadn't realised these were the last in the larder. Sam and James smiled at each other, as did the adults, other than Carter.

'Boy, you have no manners at all,' he said, and shook his head. Everyone laughed, except Leo, who still didn't understand and looked around quizzically.

'Eat, boy. Eat,' said George, and they all laughed again.

After a while, the silence was broken once more by George. He mused that there might still be a small amount of water in the 'back dam' and that it might be good enough quality to at least keep the horses going, perhaps along with a few cattle. He proposed a cart trip the next day to fill a few barrels.

'We'll just take the cart and the three boys to save water,' he said.

'I should come,' said Carter, somewhat indignantly.

'No, the boys can fit on the back and Martin and I up front. That doesn't leave a spare seat,' George answered.

The older man nodded, though he still looked disappointed. George added, 'Plus, I need you to stay here and look after the place. Who knows what that young bloke will do.'

Carter nodded again, satisfied that he would be useful.

The trip was gruelling for the three boys. The track was rough, and though they'd thrown some hessian sacks in the cart to lie on, they were still tossed from pillar to post. The idea of digging out the bottom of a muddy dam when they arrived at their destination didn't make it any easier. When they arrived, the three just silently took shovels and began to slop about in ankle-deep mud, hoping to fill the barrels as quickly as possible and get the trip back home over and done with.

They dug for about fifteen minutes, and then the two men took over. Leo and Sam sat on the edge of the dam, where most of the year, they would've been knee-deep in water. James walked to a nearby copse of wattle trees to go to the toilet. As he stood urinating at the stem of one, he noticed that two panels of the farm's rear fence had been cut and decided to investigate. When he neared the hole in the barbed wire, he could see that a wagon had travelled through the gap, and he began to follow the wheel tracks.

Back at the dam, good progress was being made, with the two men gaining some clear water, and the boys unloaded the buckets. It was hard work, but each was pleased with their input.

Suddenly, a scream made them all jump, and all tools dropped as they ran to see what could've made James emit such a bloodcurdling noise. Finding the hole in the fence, they quickly followed his tracks onto the adjoining property. They found him on his knees. The shock of what was before him had, after his initial fright, stunned him to silence.

The Sheffield rear dam was strewn with dead bodies. Not the bodies of cattle or sheep, but the bodies of Wiradjuri women and children and old men.

These were the children who the boys were playing games with in front of the fire just weeks earlier. These were the same women and elders who they'd moved from the front dam to the rear one for their own protection.

They all gasped, and Sam and Leo joined James on their knees.

Martin and George skirted the plated and dried mud, looking for survivors, finding instead the reason for their demise: stoneware bottles marked with the telling sign of the skull and crossbones. This was not an act of nature; it was an act of treachery.

The men took the boys from the scene, but they knew that no matter how fast they accomplished this, they would all be scarred for life. Seared into all of their minds was the most terrible image of all – a young mother lying dead with her still child left clinging to her breast.

Before they could move further, the warriors of the mob confronted them. They hadn't seen their fallen yet, but soon, one who'd entered the camp from another side let out a yell even more bloodcurdling than James had earlier. All flew to his side, and more screams and cries of despair rang out.

Quickly, the warriors were back on them again. Several brandished spears above their heads in threat, but one stepped between them. It was Jaiemba. He argued the other men down and stood with his own spear raised in protection of the family who'd saved his life.

The other men backed down, perhaps because of the pleading of Jaiemba, or perhaps because of the distress they could see in the three boys' faces.

All held position for a few moments. Sam moved to Jaiemba, explaining that they had just found the scene, and hadn't played any part in the murders. Jaiemba took the boy's hand in the manner of the white man, as the family had showed him. He knelt, and in one word of English, he said, 'Who?'

'We did not see,' Sam answered calmly.

Jaiemba stood and spoke a few words. It was as if the warriors were all realising that with the elders being gone, one of them became leader, and none were questioning that it would be Jaiemba. He raised his spear and they all disappeared into the nearby scrub.

They were not wasting time and burying their kin. Retribution was on their minds, and it would be swift.

Chapter 10

MARTIN AND GEORGE stood looking at each other for a few moments, deciding what they were to do. They knew not to interfere with the bodies, though they thought it abhorrent to just leave them there, unprotected, and unconsecrated in a way.

The boys huddled together on the back of the cart. None of the barrels were reloaded, as George decided to leave immediately. The tribe would be out for vengeance. He could understand their reasoning but knew he must try to stop them. The behaviour of the most extreme farmers and settlers, and even of the governor, would lead to such bad feelings that more massacres were likely if the troop retaliated. George felt that they had only been saved by Sam's connection to these people and the kindness they had always offered the troop.

Martin drove the horses hard as they headed home. He and George didn't expect that the tribe would cause any harm at their farm, but they weren't sure about other neighbours, especially those who weren't fond of the Aboriginal people, whether because of ignorance or fear.

As they arrived home, Sarah came out of the house to greet them, completely oblivious to what had happened. Seeing the distress of the boys, she hugged them to her like an old broody hen, including Leo. She looked to George for an explanation.

'They'll need to explain. We must go.' He pointed to Martin.

As the two men came out of the barn, fixing the saddles and reins of their horses, Sam said in a breaking voice, 'I should come with you.'

'There is nothing you can do now,' his father told him. 'There may be nothing anyone can do.' They rode off at a gallop.

Moving into the house, the three boys clung to Sarah, and Leo only released his grip when Carter arrived at the front door. The boy ran to him and hugged him around the waist.

'What the hell is going on?' Carter asked, looking bewildered.

'They've killed all of them,' James blurted and burst into tears.

The two men rode toward the Bathurst road as quickly as they could. Nearing the intersection, they saw a glow from the direction of the Sheffield farm, so they turned toward the east. As they approached the property's rather ostentatious gates, they could see that the homestead was on fire.

They rode hard up the approach road. Sheffield was himself staffing the buckets with several women and two old farmhands. George and Martin dived off their mounts and took the lead to try to put the flames out.

'Bloody blacks,' Sheffield cursed. 'I only got a couple of shots off. I think I hit one of them, and they all disappeared into the dark... All my men are away to the town.'

Both George and Martin could tell a tale which would explain the raid, but this wasn't the time. They fought hard and seemed to be gaining ground on the flames when two massive explosions blew away the front right-hand side of the house, as the large, ornate kerosene lamps which George and Martin had seen when they were invited into the library on their previous and only other visit ignited.

They all cowered as the flames took complete control, and Sheffield yelled, 'Buckets down,' in a broken voice. He, however, did not drop his own bucket but stood watching as his mansion was razed to the ground.

His housekeeper moved to his side, took the bucket and placed a hand on his shoulder in support. He nodded as though he understood her action, and they all moved to the veranda of the bunkhouse, to safety.

Sheffield led them. He sat on one of the long benches at the front of the building and motioned for Martin and George to join him.

'Thanks for trying to help,' he said with his head down. 'Why now, when we had just about tamed the place?'

And so, George explained the massacre at the waterhole and the group of men who'd been seen at the river the day previous. He refrained from mentioning that Sheffield Junior seemed to be their leader.

Martin was, however, not so kind, adding, 'Your young bloke was with them.'

Sheffield railed against this comment, partially to defend his son and partially because it was Martin who had made the point. 'My men would never have done this! True, I wouldn't give you tuppence for the blacks, but I would never have them kill women and children.'

His voice did not waver, and the men believed him. He paused and looked into their eyes. 'I am not a monster, you know,' he said.

Both men nodded, but secretly thought that the man in charge of the murderous mob may be.

Chapter 11

TWO MEN STOOD at the bar of the Cobb and Co station at Napoleon Reef the next evening. They were Sheffield Junior's men. The bartender was pouring drinks when the saloon-style doors burst open, and three warriors, led by Jaiemba, stood before them.

Both men went for their guns but were speared before they could even unholster them. The bartender stood for a moment and then ducked down and grabbed a blunderbuss, which he kept under the cash register. As he rose and fired, his chest was shattered by another spear. This all happened in a few moments.

The errant shot from the blunderbuss brought the bartender's wife into the saloon to investigate. As she opened the door, one of the warriors confronted her with his spear raised. She froze and then screamed as she saw her husband on the ground in a pool of blood. From behind the man, Jaiemba grabbed the spear and stopped him before he could dispatch the woman. Suddenly regaining her wits, she turned and ran, slamming the door. Bolts could be heard raking the metal clasp.

The third of Jaiemba's men had thrown one of the lamps, and the saloon was now on fire. Jaiemba signalled and they left as quickly as they had entered.

Two men who'd been lodging in the overhead rooms heard the

woman's screams and came bounding down the stairs in various stages of undress, but both had pistols drawn. The woman added to the arsenal by retrieving another blunderbuss which was kept in the kitchen, and as she tried to explain what was happening, they positioned themselves near the rear entrance.

All three were reluctant to open the door, but after around a minute, which seemed like an hour, one of the men turned the handle and crept out. There was no sound audible for a few moments, except for the noise of the fire and the panicked animals in the barn. The heat from the fire, which had now engulfed the entire front half of the building, drove them to escape through the open door. No further violence was committed, though one of the men fired a shot in fright as the saw the reflection of the flames in a horse water trough.

The bartender was the only man killed who had taken no part in the massacre, but he had fired a shot, which had to be met.

The fact that the warriors did not kill the woman was quickly forgotten. When the story hit the streets of Bathurst the next day, many a man echoed the thoughts of the Governor of New South Wales during the Bathurst Plains War, that 'they are little more than animals – why not kill them all?'

George and Martin argued against that sentiment. George stood on one of the street corners and explained to a large group of men, who were preparing a militia to chase down and kill as many 'blacks' as they could, what had started the violence. Several of the men changed their minds when George spoke, and women and other older men standing as spectators around the crowd clapped as he made points about all men being born equal.

When he highlighted that there were many outlying stations which would be in peril if the violence spread to more Wiradjuri, or the other tribes, several more people who had friends and relatives on such stations shouted their support.

From the crowd, a voice came which Martin and George recognised. 'Black lover!'

The throng turned toward the voice. It was Sheffield Junior.

'Your behaviour may well be the cause of this violence,' George fired back at him.

'While white people are dying and my own father's farm is razed to the ground, you still talk of peace!' the young man shouted, and some hoots were heard from the men who stood around him.

'When they are left in peace, they're a fine people. When they are under attack, they retaliate,' George countered.

'Perhaps you should look after your own,' the young man shouted.

'Those who murder women and children need give me little advice,' George quipped angrily, and the people nearest Sheffield murmured, moving where they could out of the line of fire.

'You take that back, or I'll have you in court!' Sheffield shouted, losing his cool.

'I don't believe I mentioned any names, but if you put your hand up...' George shouted back, and the crowd again made disapproving noises.

Sheffield knew that he was losing more than he was winning and so resorted to getting his men to start a chant of, 'Black lover, black lover, black lover!' Enough people joined in to make it impossible for George's words of honour and peace to be heard.

'Who's with me?' Sheffield shouted, and he and around half the men who had originally joined the vigilante group mounted their horses and rode off, continuing the chant.

When they had left, those who stood around looked lost, but George again spoke in a low, calm but loud enough voice to be heard. 'Keep faith; you have made the right decision. There is no need to exterminate these people.'

He paused and waited for silence, and for those who had turned away to look back. 'I saw the waterhole which had been poisoned and the elders, women and children lying where they fell.' His voice quavered for a moment, and a tear streaked his cheek. 'I saw those women, some with child, and one with an infant still clinging to her... all dead, and the poison bottles in the mud.'

He paused again. 'In humanity's name, no man, woman or child deserves to be treated like this.'

A soft round of applause waved round the crowd, which now numbered more than fifty. Women cried and huddled together, never having heard the truth of how the local tribes were treated.

'What can *we* do?' one of the women said. George and Martin recognised her as Madam Sophie.

'We must see the mayor and captain and let them know that we don't want a bloodbath.'

'You should speak for us,' said the general store proprietor George Adam James, who everyone in the town called G.A. The crowded mass murmured their approval.

'Happy to help, but I think a large group of people descending on the mayoral chamber would make a more lasting impression,' George answered.

Martin was clapping his support, but his eyes hadn't left the shrouded woman who stood next to Madam Sophie. There was something familiar in her movement and the shape of her chin, which was the only part of her face visible.

'Let's go, then,' said one of the men.

G.A. rejoined with, 'Yes, we are with you, Douglas.'

The crowd crossed the road, Martin still watching the woman. They all walked to the mayoral office and completely covered the road and both footpaths. George knocked on the door, and the mayor's secretary and wife opened it. She was very much taken aback by the mass of people in front of her.

'We would like to see Harley,' George said.

The woman, dumbfounded, closed the door. In a few minutes, the dishevelled, half-dressed figure of Mayor Harley Williams emerged. It was obvious that he had still been in bed. Perhaps sleeping off one of his long sessions with the bottle.

'What the hell is going on?' he spluttered and then, seeing one of the women, said, 'Pardon me, ma'am.'

George stepped forward and spoke so the whole crowd could hear him. 'There has been a terrible massacre of the local Wiradjuri. All the elders, women and children were murdered. They were poisoned at the waterhole at the far north of the Sheffield property.' He waited for the crowd's murmur of support.

'The men of the tribe were not with them, but having seen what was done, they have gone on a rampage. They've burned the Sheffield house down and killed two men at Napoleon Reef. Should we wish to live safely in our own homes, we need to have some form of agreement with the tribes, and not always be at war with them.'

'If we wipe them out, they won't be burning houses,' put in Harley.

'But there will always be more of them. Who knows how many there are out west?' George countered. 'It may be you who is caught while out visiting your constituents,' he added, knowing full well that the mayor never visited anyone unless there was some financial advantage to be gained.

'This is not the time or place to discuss such things,' Harley said, annoyed by this slight.

'Sure, only talk about them when the rest of the town can't hear, so none of the women can hear! We need action now!' shouted Madam Sophie.

'Madam, when you run for town council, you can be present at the meetings,' he scolded.

'If I were allowed to, I would, but perhaps we have found our next mayor here in Mr Douglas,' she shouted back angrily, and the crowd whooped and hollered in agreement.

'I take that as a personal insult,' Harley blurted.

'Good! You understood me, then, in your delicate state,' she came straight back at him, and the crowd all laughed uproariously.

'You are no lady!' he yelled back, completely losing his composure.

'Tell us something we don't know,' Sophie quipped, obviously enjoying the sport. The crowd all laughed again.

After waiting for the uproar to die down a bit, she added, 'Now get off your pickled rump and do something.'

'What would you have me do?' He sneered at her.

George saw his chance to intercede here, knowing that the mayor was no match for the madam, even if he was sober.

'I think we should send a deputation to the captain to let him know what has happened. We should ask him to try to settle things down with the Wiradjuri if he can and to stop that mob,' he said and was roundly supported.

'I would not presume to tell Captain Allen what to do,' said the mayor, still reeling.

'No, we have no right to, but we could make suggestions. After all, they are here to protect us and our ability to feed the colony,' George said, knowing Harley got a fee for every load of food which was carted to Sydney.

'I could go and speak to Allen,' Harley finally conceded.

One member of the crowd shouted that they wanted George to accompany him, and Harley again bristled up. 'That man has no authority to represent anyone.'

'He might have at the next election,' shouted another man standing at the rear of the assembly. Laughter again rippled across the now more than seventy people who'd poured out of all the businesses on the street.

'Oh, alright, I'll go with you, Douglas, but it will be of no use. Allen will do away with them as well,' Harley concluded sulkily.

'We'll at least try to make him listen,' said George, and he took Harley's arm and began to half-drag the tipsy man to Captain Allen's office.

The crowd gave them a send-off cheer and began to break up. Madam Sophie walked with her offsider toward the business for which she was renowned, and they were followed, at a distance, by Martin. He was sure he knew the person with her, and he intended to find out if he was correct. He waited until both had entered the front door and gave it a moment before knocking.

Madam Sophie opened the door and, immediately recognising him, said, 'Mr Martin.' She always called her punters 'Mr', and then their first name. This allowed them some kind of privacy, while everyone really knew who they were. 'You're a bit early for the girls today.'

'I'm not looking to see the girls. Just one,' he answered.

'Oh, and which one would that be?' she asked.

'The girl you just came in with.'

'No, you don't want to see her. She's not one of the working girls, not at all.'

'What is her name?' he persisted.

'They call her Cicatrix,' Sophie answered softly.

'I need to see her.'

'You won't like what you see,' she answered him, calling the girl to her side. Her face was swathed in lace, and she looked at the ground, but the eyes – the eyes were the giveaway.

'Willow?' he said as a question, and then, as a slight lifting of the eyes came in acknowledgement, 'Willow,' he repeated, as a statement.

Then came a silent standoff for a few moments, eventually broken as he said, in a deep and calm voice, 'You can't hide from me; I've been looking for you since we were children. Since I got this, "Cicatrix".' He ran his finger along the length of the scar on his face.

Another silence ensued. Eventually, Martin swept her up in his arms and removed the lace. She attempted to cover her face, but he stilled her hand and said, 'You're as beautiful now as I remember.

Neither Draper nor any other man could ever take that away from you.'

She pushed him away and recovered her veil.

'You must be mistaken, darlin',' Sophie put in.

'It doesn't matter. Nothing matters. I love you; I have always loved you,' he persisted and swept Willow up in his arms again. This time, she did not resist, and they kissed through the veil.

'Bloody hell!' exclaimed Sophie.

'You must come with me now,' Martin insisted.

'No. There's a job I have to do here first,' Willow said and withdrew from his arms.

'You don't owe me anything, dear,' Sophie said. 'I'm always happy when some man takes one of my girls away, but I never guessed you would be the next.'

She put a reassuring hand on the nearest shoulder of both as they stood looking at each other.

'Trust me. There's a job I need to finish,' the girl reiterated.

'I don't understand,' Martin babbled. 'I love you.'

The lace dropped from a very sallow face.

'He's here!' she said in a lifeless voice, and Martin knew exactly who 'he' was.

Chapter 12

A SMATTERING OF light danced on the kitchen table. It was dawn, and Sam and James's heads rested on placemats next to each other. They had slept there overnight, waiting for their father to arrive home.

No message, no word at all, had come from Bathurst. They knew that their father and Martin would be in grave danger if they'd followed the troop to try to reason with them. The boys knew nothing of the two fires, or the men who'd been killed, but still resting, just at arm's length, were their rifles.

Sarah sat in the corner with her rifle across her lap. She had been there, watching over her distraught sons, all through the night. It had been years since she'd seen them both cry openly together.

They had told her the basics of what they'd found, though they would go no further than a brief outline. Sarah didn't have the heart to push them for any detail, and indeed, she probably didn't want to know the gore, the terror, which had torn them both apart.

Leo was in his room. Carter sat beside his bed with a double-barrelled shotgun. The boy had also fallen asleep at the table, but he was small enough to be carried to his room.

Carter was basically a passive man, though he had lived in Arizona in North America, and had had to take the life of a young Navajo brave to escape a scouting party. He felt neither proud nor settled about what he had done. Soon after the killing, he had journeyed to Australia, knowing there was much less fighting, and less chance he would have to bear arms.

This family he had fallen in with was so giving and loving that he felt it was only right to help protect them and Leo. The boy at his side had attached himself to Carter after the man had found him sleeping rough with no food in a life-threatening condition on the outskirts of Parramatta. They had travelled to the Walker property over the Blue Mountains at Wallerowang. James Walker himself gave them both shelter and labour as he completed his second homestead.

They'd spent eighteen months on general construction and handyman work. Walker had found a loophole in the property ownership laws in the relatively new colony. Unclaimed land of two thousand acres was deemed to be owned if a free settler or ex-convict built a working homestead on the land. Walker set about putting a manager in charge at Wallerowang and moved his sights to the Wolgan Valley, where he built another homestead.

Walker had usually been a good judge of character, though the man he had placed in charge of the station was not pleasant. As the drought hit, the manager dismissed almost all of the workers who'd helped build a second building, a large barn. He quickly replaced them with members of his own family or his closest cronies. This set Carter, Leo and fifteen other workers adrift, with no hope of work in the immediate area. Almost all the men, including Carter and Leo, walked to Bathurst, the only large town inland which was close enough to reach on foot.

There, they found little work and little food. Now, with the Douglases, they were sure of three meals a day and a safe bed. Aware that Walker would go out of his way to meet and be generous to the local Wiradjuri people, Carter knew what fine people they were. Indeed, one mob had fed him and Leo on their way to Wallerowang, James Walker's property, while they were passing through the Hartley valley. They had received much less help from some settlers in the area.

While Carter thought of these things, Leo stirred a little, and he covered the boy's shoulder with his blanket. These times had changed him, and he would now fight to the death to protect the family.

Horses entered the yard, travelling slowly. Sarah was up at the front window in a flash. Seeing George mounted and three other horses, she rushed onto the veranda, placing her rifle behind the front door. James followed her, though he still bore his weapon.

Behind George was Martin, then a veiled lady, mounted side-saddle, and the fourth horse was covered by a somewhat dishevelled Sheffield. Sarah pounced on George and kissed him when his feet had hardly hit the ground; she clung to him as he introduced their guests. James held the reins for the lady so she might dismount. He also took Martin's reins but not those of their other visitor. This was meant to be a slight, but no one seemed to notice.

'Darling, Mr Sheffield's home has been burned, and he will need to stay a few days in the bunkhouse,' he said. Sarah nodded her understanding. 'And this is the girl Martin and I grew up with, Willow.'

Sarah moved quickly to Willow and hugged her. She knew why she wore the veil, remembering the story George and Martin had told her.

'My dear,' she said, 'how wonderful to meet you. I feel like we're old friends; George and Martin have told us about you so many times.'

She turned to Sheffield. 'Mr Sheffield, you are my husband's guest, and I welcome you to stay as long as you need to.' She was obviously not as delighted to see him.

Sam had stirred and now exited the front door, followed by Carter and Leo.

'Stable the horses, boys,' ordered George, and the three of them rushed to take the reins and move the steeds into the stable.

The boys unsaddled each and gave them a quick brush down. As they led the horses to their stalls, Sam blurted, 'Who is the woman, and why is Sheffield here?'

'He's here because Jaiemba and his men burned the Sheffield house down,' James answered.

'Good,' said Sam, and the three boys looked at each other and nodded, each thinking it was the least Jaiemba could do.

'And the dame?' questioned Leo.

'I didn't catch her name, but she's a friend of father and Martin,' James answered, smiling at the term 'dame', which he and Sam would never think to use.

After they'd finally secured the four horses and begun to fill their feed boxes, Martin appeared at the door with a glass of wine in his hand. 'Sit down with me, men,' he said. 'These are hard times, and Old

Man Sheffield will have to stay with us for a few days, so we need you all to be civil to him.'

Leo had no idea why they would not be 'civil' to him, whatever that meant. The two sitting to his right understood exactly why. They, like Martin and George, suspected Sheffield Junior had orchestrated the massacre, perhaps at his father's bidding.

Sam took a breath as if he was about to speak, but Martin raised his hand and said, 'Yes, yes, I know, but that is the way it is, and we shall all just have to put up with it.'

'You see this scar?' He pointed to the mark, which still, these many years on, branded his cheek, red and twisted. They all nodded. It was hard to miss.

'You've heard plenty of tall tales as to how I got it.' They all nodded again. 'Now I'm going to tell you the truth.'

He took a deep breath. 'Many years ago, when your father and I were very young, we were sent to an orphanage. We grew up there with our greatest friend Willow, the lady you saw arrive tonight. We were very poor and starving before going to the orphanage, and once there, we at least had two feeds a day.'

He paused for effect. 'A very evil man named Draper worked there as a housemaster. He hated your father and me and used to beat us whenever he could. He hated everyone, really.'

The boys hung onto every word. They had heard so many stories from Martin and were never sure where fact and fiction parted.

'One day, he went mad and attacked me and your father. Another housemaster, Gibson, came to save us, and Draper pulled a knife.'

Suddenly, the boys realised this wasn't one of the tall tales they were used to. This was violent and seemed too real.

'He slashed me down, and I never saw properly what happened next. All I know is that your father was badly hurt, and Gibson was also stabbed. One of the girls' governesses was knocked down, and her hip was broken. Somewhere among all of that, my darling Willow was slashed across the face, and like me, she bears the scars to this day.'

He halted for a moment. A tear snaked its way down his cheek and left his scar glistening.

'They took her away,' he said in a sad voice. He breathed deeply again. 'She would not see me, and your father and I had never spoken to her again until yesterday.' He lowered his head as another tear followed the track of the first.

James and Sam looked at each other, and Leo switched glances between them, not knowing what to say, if anything.

'You love her?' Sam said, awkwardly breaking the silence. His query was met by a nod; Martin could not find any words.

'If you love her, we will love her,' James, ever the politician, reassured him, and placed his hand on Martin's shoulder.

Young men weren't usually expected to show physical affection at this time. The social norms were broken, however, as Leo stood and hugged Martin. Sam and James in turn shook his hand, and all wiped away the 'unmanly' tears.

As the party entered the house, they could see Willow sitting next to Sarah. Her face was still covered, and Sarah held her hand, showing how truly delighted she was to meet Martin and George's childhood friend. George stood with his back to the open fire, and Carter had retired to his room.

Sam moved first. He crossed the room and sat at his mother's right hand on the large couch. Martin moved to stand with George, and the other two boys sat on the floor near Martin's feet, warming their hands.

Sarah, always one to break an awkward silence, said, 'How long have you been in the colony?'

After a short time, Willow answered. 'I've been here for two and a half years, most of that time in Queensland. I've only been in Bathurst for two weeks,' she added, foreseeing Sarah's next question.

'Could you boys get some wood in and set the table for breakfast?' George asked.

Sarah added, as the three left the room, 'Light the stove as well, please.'

The boys obeyed, knowing this was intended to allow some 'adult time'.

As soon as the youngsters had left, Martin came and sat next to Willow. There wasn't much room left on the couch at that end, and Sarah had to move along. Martin took Willow's hand and held it. Obviously, he never wanted to let her go again.

'Tell us your story, Willow. How did you come to be here?' asked Sarah.

Willow did not immediately answer but turned her eyes toward Martin. He nodded his approval, and she timidly began.

'I grew up with "Mother Marshall", as I called her, and her sister Mrs Skinner. Both had become widows early in life, but Nell Skinner had married a banker from Scotland, and his investments meant that we were never in need.' She took a long, slow breath. 'Nell passed about five years ago, and Mother six months later to the day. She had left everything to me, and though I was not rich, it was a substantial amount. The cottage and a small dressmaker's shop were also placed in my name. I had plied my trade there and been taught all manner of needlecraft. I'd taken to embroidery and sold many pieces over the years.'

Willow pressed her hands together. 'The two widows brought a master embroider out from London once a month to teach me anything I couldn't learn from books. He declared me to have completed my apprenticeship after three years, and I was employed to create large wall hangings under his direction for several years. To some, this was a craft of days gone by, but to the wealthy, they were the greatest of artworks.'

She bent forward and lifted the cup of tea which sat in front of her, held the veil aside a little and took a sip. Placing the cup back on the table, she continued, 'Every couple of months, a cart would arrive at the shop to take away completed work and bring my new commissions. This was a wonderful outlet for me. My art was renowned, though I was still never seen in public. One day around two or three years ago, the cart arrived with a different driver. As soon as I saw him, I went into the storeroom, returned with the blunderbuss originally kept by Nell, and shot him.'

'Oh, my dear,' gasped Sarah and moved back a little, startled.

'He used a different name, but it was him. I knew him immediately. He fell over backwards.' She paused again, though she did not seem upset, nor did she breathe more deeply as she resumed her story. 'Unfortunately, the gun was loaded with saltpetre, which Nell would fire toward the cats who occasionally approached our dovecot. He got up when he realised he wasn't dead and clutched at his chest where the shot had struck him. He was about to shout something when I tore off my veil. As he saw my face, a sudden realisation seemed to come to him. He turned and ran like the coward he always was. I followed him into the street and pulled the trigger several more times. While he gained his seat on the wagon and whipped the horses, I continued to pull the trigger, though to no avail, as it was a one-shot affair. The wagon tore off down the street, and then he was gone, and I came to my senses.'

Her listeners sat in complete silence, hardly daring to blink.

'The butcher and several other men came to my aid, taking the gun and laying me on the bench in front of the shop. The butcher's wife took care of me, dabbing my face with water until I regained my sanity fully, and reattached the veil.'

Now breathing quite quickly, she continued, 'It had been years, years of torture, seeing his face whenever I slept. I knew I could not let him go, and though those around me kept asking what he had done, I could not articulate it well enough to have them understand.'

She looked to Martin and then to George. 'It was Draper,' she said, and her veiled eyes filled with tears.

Sarah immediately hugged her, and though Martin moved to do the same, Sarah did not let go. She looked up to George and saw real tears flowing down his cheeks. She knew that this Draper must be the man whom she had been told about, the man George had called 'the evil creature at the orphanage'. She stood and moved to him, taking his hand. Then, as was her way when times were at their worst, she hugged him.

Willow sat solemnly watching them, then cringed a little as Martin drew her to him. After a moment, she acquiesced, and several minutes passed with each in their loved one's arms.

Suddenly, Willow spoke again, not having finished the story. 'I travelled the next day to London and visited the company which had sent Draper. They informed me that the mongrel had not returned the previous day and that they had people out looking for him. I waited at the office until they were closing but nothing was heard of him.'

She took a long, slow breath through her nose, then continued. 'The next day, I learned that he had gone to his sister's home, taken all of his goods and all her money, and left. It took another three weeks to find out where he'd gone. He'd signed on to the *Eliza II*, bound for Port Macquarie, New South Wales, Australia.'

Another awkward moment passed, and this time, it was Martin who spoke. 'It doesn't matter... You're here now,' he said, his voice faltering.

'So is he!' she answered coldly. 'I sold everything for much less than it was worth and booked passage to Australia. I arrived in Brisbane and found that Draper had stuck with the ship as it moved to Fiji and that the boat would go to New Zealand and on to Sydney. So, I booked a ticket on a transport ship to follow him to Sydney.'

Her fixed glare, though covered, investigated the distance.

'I was there when he landed, and I followed him to a boarding house at the rocks, where he booked in for the night. I went and booked a room and thought about how I could deal with him. Then, the very next day, I heard that he had left for Bathurst and parts further west to prospect for gold. The only way I had to follow him was via Cobb and Co, so I set out two days later.'

'How did you end up with Miss Sophie?' asked George.

'I got off the coach to find that my luggage was missing, with much of my money, and Sophie saw me outside the store sitting on a box trying to decide what to do next. She came and spoke to me, and I realised quickly what she was, and what she was offering me. I opened my veil, and she said, "Well, I need a housekeeper and a secretary, if you can write?" I was surprised and told her that she didn't need to pay me, as I would pay my own way.'

She rolled her head from side to side to settle the soreness in her neck. 'We became such good friends that she asked if I was following a man and I said yes. I think she knew that my scars weren't new, but she asked if a lover had done this to me. I told her the whole story, and she offered to help; she's a wonderful soul and thought what I had done and was going to do was only right.'

She paused again. 'She had a little joke with me when she called me Miss Cicatrix. Though I wasn't that impressed at first, I got over it in the five weeks I stayed with her and came to really trust her.'

'But, my dear, what were you going to do?' questioned Sarah.

'I was, and I am, going to kill him,' she answered plainly, with her eyes fixed on that faraway goal.

Sarah looked up at George and wondered if he and Martin felt the same. That night, when they'd all retired, she asked George what he thought about the idea of Willow killing Draper. He took quite a while to answer, as he hadn't even given the idea a second thought.

Slowly and thoughtfully, he pondered his response, then he said, 'I fear that Draper has driven her to madness.'

Sarah watched his face, silhouetted by the candle on the bedside table.

'I asked what you thought,' she pressed.

He again chose his words carefully, then answered, 'I can see why she wants what she wants. He ruined her life and left Martin unable to make friends or trust anyone.'

'And you?' she asked.

'What do you want me to say? Yes, I would like to see him dead. He doesn't deserve to live. Would I kill him? I have you and the boys to think about, so no, I wouldn't.'

There was a pause while he thought. 'I haven't met him in the street, though. If I did, I think I'd have to hit him.'

George noticed her eyebrows rise and added, 'He's an animal. He shouldn't be allowed to live among good people after he did what he did.'

He held himself back again, seeing that she was surprised by his vehement answer.

'I promise I will not lift a hand against him if I can control myself,' he said. 'However, I will not stop Martin, or her, if they plan his end.'

Sarah moved closer to him. He often seemed like a little boy when uncertain of himself, and she could certainly tell he was uncertain now.

The next morning, Martin met George in the stables, where he'd been working for some time. He was an early riser normally; today, though, he was up hours before the sun.

'I thought I could hear you out here,' Martin said, expecting an answer, but none came. He began to assist in the feeding of the horses, and eventually, the silence was broken by his friend.

'It won't do, all this talk of killing Draper,' he said, turning to look at Martin.

'It's not just talk,' Martin answered, continuing with the work and deliberately not making eye contact.

'What do you mean to do?' George asked shortly.

'We mean to find him and kill him,' came the answer, in a matter-of-fact way.

'You will both hang,' George fired back, hoping still to talk some sense into his friend.

'We don't really care; he will pay at last,' Martin said, still in a detached voice.

George turned to him, took both his shoulders, and shook him once. 'Control yourself, man!'

Martin now looked him square in the eyes. 'I am in complete control, and I feel the best I have for years.'

George let go with a shocked look on his face, not knowing what to say next.

'He destroyed our lives, and he will pay,' Martin assured him.

'How are you going to do it?' he asked.

'However it comes, and wherever we find him,' Martin answered with a sallow smile.

George stared at him incredulously for a moment, and then Martin moved away to saddle his mount.

George stood for a time, then left the stable, intent on talking to Willow. However, when he entered the house, he found her eating breakfast with Sarah and the three boys. He sat down at the head of the table, and soon after, Carter sat beside him. They all ate well, though Willow only took some toasted damper with butter and placed it into her mouth under her veil.

'What is England like now?' James broke the silence, addressing Willow.

She looked into his eyes for a moment, then realised he was actually interested in what she had to say and wasn't just paying lip service to good manners.

'Well, there's never enough food for most, and it can be very cold, not like here,' she answered.

'Which do you rather?' the boy persisted.

'I love the weather here and the wide-open spaces,' she answered honestly.

Sam joined the discussion, asking, 'Is London as big as Father says?'

'It's too big. There are too many people. Sometimes, I thought I would never get out of the place.' She stared at the three boys who sat opposite her and thought how wonderful they were, how wonderful it was that they never had to go through what she, Martin and George had. Wonderful that they had the parents they did, and wonderful that they lived in this warm, beautiful place.

'That's enough now, boys. Finish your breakfast and get about your chores,' Sarah said, interpreting Willow's faraway look. She needed to be alone with Willow.

The boys were all well-mannered, and immediately did what they were told, eating quietly.

Sarah placed a cup of tea next to Willow and another in front of herself, putting her hand on the other woman's as she was thanked.

'A good cup of tea helps start the day,' she said, hoping the small talk would get Willow ready for the real talk.

They sat for a few minutes, and then Willow broke the awkward silence, saying, 'What beautiful young men you have. They're a credit to you.'

'They would be if they got about their chores,' Sarah answered. The boys smiled as they finished and left the room.

The two women retired to the lounge room and sat by the large, crackling fire.

'I'm glad we're alone,' Sarah said and continued in a stern tone, 'but this business about killing people, how can you say that?'

'I know what you must think of me,' Willow answered, pulling away her veil. 'He did this, and he will die.'

Sarah showed no horror, which had been Willow's intended reaction, but simply said, 'I know what he did to you both, and to George, but surely the law must do something?'

'There is no law, no justice, and he will pay,' Willow concluded bitterly. She rose and exited the room.

Sarah had wanted to talk the problem out. However, she could see now that was something only Martin could do, and it was obvious he had no intent to do anything of the sort.

Martin had entered the kitchen and sat silently with the other two men, who were eating. He could tell that things were tense. The air was thick. Sarah came back into the room and said to Martin, 'What would you like for breakfast? Eggs, bacon?'

'That would be lovely,' he answered.

Carter and George had finished their food. Both got up and left the kitchen, bound for the vegetable patch, the chore for the morning.

'While I have you here, I wanted to ask about this pact to kill Draper,' Sarah said.

'Yes?' questioned Martin.

'Well, you must see that it's wrong?' she asked, looking him in the eye and delivering his plate of food.

'I don't believe it's wrong,' he answered shortly.

Sarah, wide eyed, stuttered, 'I-I don't see how you can think of doing it?'

'I don't understand how you can question this. He is evil. He ruined both our lives, and he must pay.'

Sarah paused a moment, then with greater resolve, said, 'I won't have this in my house. The boys, and especially George, must have no part in this. Do you understand?'

'Dear Sarah, I do understand. I will not mention it to the boys, and George wouldn't be welcome in our plan. We alone will make him pay.' He paused a moment and then said, in a somewhat condescending voice, 'I thank you for making Willow feel welcome. She hasn't had that in her life much.'

'I understand why you feel you must do this,' she said, ignoring his last comment. 'I wish you didn't.'

Martin stood and gave her a small kiss on the cheek, then exited without another word. Little did she know that the newly rejoined couple had decided to take the cart into Bathurst the next day to find Draper and do away with him. Aware that they would both hang, they had also decided to take their own lives and end the whole affair.

Ridiculous decisions are made in haste, and this was an ill-thought-out plan. What if Draper got the drop on them, or someone else got in the way? What gain was there to be had?

When Martin asked to borrow the cart, George didn't even ask why. He knew his friend well and was sure that he and Willow were going to confront their foe. He could not bring himself to stop them, or even try to talk Martin around. That had never borne fruit before, and he knew that it would not work now. Martin had his soulmate back.

Chapter 13

GEORGE DECIDED TO go across land and into Bathurst to see if he could warn Draper off, hoping to find the man first. Making good time, he reached the outskirts of the town well ahead of the cart. He immediately moved to the Black Bull Bar, which he knew a more questionable clientele frequented. The bartender would tell him nothing, but as he exited, a drunk assailed him on the front veranda, saying he knew where Draper could be found.

George knew the man was begging for drinking funds, and though he had no desire for his coin to be wasted on grog, he crossed the man's palm with two shillings and was told to go to the diggings near Winburndale.

Winburndale was a high area where a large group of miners had set up a rough camp, close to the many diggings on the side of the hill. Men would dig all day and draw out whatever gold they could find then spend it at the camp, buying food and supplies from Roman Johnson, who had set up a tawdry tent and wagon full of cheap knick-knacks and basic food, which he made available to the inhabitants from the goodness of his heart and for the improvement of his pocket.

Johnson had always been called 'Roman'. No one was ever quite sure whether it was actually his name or an indirect slight at the profile of his nose. They all knew, however, if there was a penny to be made,

Roman would have his tendrils wrapped around part of the take.

According to the drunk, Draper had, like so many of his fellow diggers, started by purchasing one of the already formed tunnels which pocked the hillside from a group of men headed by Roman. There may be gold in the hills, or there may be none, but the consortium took the initial outlay and twenty-five percent of any ore found without even lifting a pick or shovel.

George knew Roman, as did everyone in the frontier town. George had made his acquaintance through extraordinary church meetings: burials, christenings, and the like. Neither would have considered themselves, or the other, a religious man. It just seemed that they each knew the people who were dying or being born.

As soon as Roman was mentioned, George felt that his chance of finding Draper before Martin and Willow was good. He would stump up the recommended donation and have the information as soon as was humanly possible.

Cantering as much as he thought his mount could bear, George crossed the Bathurst Plains going east and headed up the mountain. Hardly a person was to be seen in the camp, though as many as one hundred and fifty rough shanties and tents covered the area and made it look untidy.

Riding directly to Roman's 'establishment', George was met by one of the man's handlers. A big bruiser of Middle European appearance with an accent to match.

'What you want?' he growled, as though his very important work had been interrupted.

'Roman,' George answered, and the man appeared as if by magic from behind a dirty red and black curtain.

'Yes, Mr Douglas?' he said quietly, waving the henchman away.

George knew that this was not a place for honest men to dwell and quickly stated his business. 'I would like to know the whereabouts of a man going by the name Draper,' he said.

'Perhaps this Draper does not wish to be found?' the crook said, rubbing his hands together.

'I'm sure he will be anxious to meet with me.' George reached for his wallet.

'As anxious as the two people who were here earlier, do you think?' the man asked, smiling broadly like the cat who'd got the cream.

'Quickly, man, what's your price?'

As they moved closer to each other, two troopers could be heard riding up the last part of the incline, as if they'd followed George.

'Gentlemen.' Brushing George aside, Roman moved to stand before the two riders. Bowing deeply, he added, 'How can I help you?'

The leading rider shifted in his saddle and said in a condescending tone, 'Enough of your shit, we're 'ere for the man Draper.' His face was grim as he looked down on Roman both actually and figuratively.

'A very popular man today, this Draper,' Roman answered him.

'Where will we find 'im?' the mounted man persisted.

'I should take you there,' Roman said, and his offsider appeared with a saddled horse, as if he had been preparing for a quick departure. He mounted, and George, seeing his chance, moved quickly to his horse and did the same.

It was obvious that Roman knew the quickest way to the Draper mineshaft. As they skirted a grove of trees and some heath near the highest point of the plateau, they could see the shape of a man near a small campfire, sitting on a gnarled tree stump. They could also see, approaching from the road a full fifty yards down the hill, Martin and Willow. Roman had obviously given them a circuitous route in his directions.

'Draper!' The leading trooper called in a loud, clear voice, and Draper jumped, completely startled. Getting to his feet, he glanced to where the voice had come from, and spotting the mounted troopers, George, and Roman, he turned away from them. Then he saw Martin and Willow blocking his downhill retreat. Feeling as though he was surrounded, he took to his heel and ran across the slope away from the troopers, sprinting at full pelt. Draper had a horse of his own but had left it to graze on a nearby open field, and he was trying to get to it and simply flee. He wasn't sure what he was running from, but he'd done enough wrongs in his time to understand that the troopers weren't there for a social visit.

The chase was on, and George and the troopers rode hard to cut off Draper's escape, though it seemed as if Roman had lost interest. He just sat on his mount without moving. Martin also began to run below the fleeing man, though across and up the slope. Willow, encumbered by a full dress, could only move as fast as the garment would allow. Subsequently, she fell well behind Martin and even lost sight of him for a few moments.

Draper knew the lay of the land better than his pursuers, and though he was not mounted, it looked as though he may make the washaway which split the 'south diggings' from the 'north diggings'. Seeing his intent, one of the troopers made a serious effort to get there first, which he achieved just moments before the felon.

Draper, hemmed in, turned to go down the steep side of the hill and fell. He bounced once and tumbled out of view. The slope was too steep to follow. There was an overhanging rock ledge at least one hundred yards across, and no one could get close enough to the edge to see Draper's fate.

Willow had seen the dreaded man drop, but like the others, she realised the men above would have to backtrack to get to the lower level on which she and Martin had arrived. She began to run back toward the cart. Martin also tracked backwards, and though he could move faster than Willow, he was a long way behind when she mounted the cart and tapped the horse to get him into a trot.

Roman, who'd seen everything, had moved his mount steadily down the hill. He was just behind the cart as he made the lower level. Martin fell in some forty or fifty yards behind him, and the troopers and George had to go back the full length of the escarpment and so were not in sight.

As Willow rounded the corner of the lower road, she could see, some twenty meters above, the limp body of her lifelong adversary.

The fall would most likely have killed any man, but Draper had landed across a huge piece of broken timber and was impaled through his midriff and chest. The sight was gruesome and drove Willow to madness; she could not believe the bastard was gone. She had been robbed of the chance of revenge. Her eyes glared, and she pulled a revolver from her gown and took aim at the lifeless body.

Roman arrived and dismounted just as she settled her aim and, thrusting his hand upwards, made sure that the shot flew harmlessly into the air. He took the weapon from her as she swooned into his arms in a dead faint.

As he laid her on the ground, Martin arrived and fell on his knees at her side. George and the lead trooper came next to the scene, and the trooper enquired why Roman, who stood with the pistol in hand, had fired.

Thinking quickly, the man answered, 'I wanted to let you know where we were.'

'What?' the trooper asked incredulously.

'I was startled and fired to summon help,' Roman stuttered and pointed to the body of Draper.

The second trooper arrived and, looking up, exclaimed, 'Oh my God!'

George knelt beside Willow and Martin and gave the woman a light shake, though she did not respond. The two troopers dismounted and stood either side of Roman, staring up at the awful sight.

'How will we get him down?' the subordinate asked.

'Go back to Roman's camp and bring me some men with axes,' his senior barked. 'Take him with you, and take that bloody gun from him.' He pointed at the pistol in Roman's hand.

The two men did as ordered, and the lead trooper joined the other pair at Willow's side.

'What was this all about?' he asked.

George looked up, the glint of a tear in his eye, and said, 'We were just coming to see Draper; we knew him from the old country.'

The trooper paused for a moment, still looking at Willow, and then asked, 'Why were you looking for him? He was to be arrested. Miss Sophie and two of her girls had brought charges against him... He seems to have been a very violent man.'

Never a truer word was spoken, George thought, but only nodded his head.

Willow began to come round. 'Draper, dead,' she babbled, with other words which would remain indecipherable to the three men.

George quickly helped Martin lift her. They moved to the back of the cart and carefully placed her in the tray, making sure that her head rested on some hay. Martin joined her. George collected his horse and took the driver's seat, having tied his mount to the buckboard.

'We'll take her directly to the doctor,' he said, the comment directed at the trooper, who just nodded his acquiescence.

Chapter 14

THE CART PULLED up in front of the doctor's office. Willow had continued to babble, and Martin had continued to comfort her. Once inside, she was placed on a treatment table, and the doctor's wife forced the two men from the room so Doctor West could examine her.

'What brought the attack on?' Mrs West asked them, looking over her wire-rimmed glasses as she took her seat at the desk in the waiting room.

'She witnessed a man falling off a cliff,' George answered.

Mrs West, taking notes, raised an eyebrow and said in a condescending tone, 'Well, that'll do it, she'll be in shock. She'll need to stay with us for a couple of days.'

'Her name is Willow, and she is to be my wife.' Martin broke his silence, snapping at her obnoxious attitude.

The old woman lifted her gaze and glared at him as if disgusted that she had to deal with the likes of these people. She was a lady of some breeding. She received as strong and as disgusted a glare in return; Martin had dealt with bullying upper-class curs all his life, and he recognised the woman in front of him as another of that ilk.

'How much money do you want?' George cut in with a calmer voice, hoping that the word 'money' would interest her. It did.

'Two shillings for board and another for drugs.' She continued with a smile, 'If there's anything else, we can settle it when you come to pick her up, um, next Sunday.' She wrote in the diary in front of her, then slammed it, as if to complete the transaction.

George knew she was overcharging but took three shillings from his fob pocket and placed them on the table. He was amazed by the speed with which she scooped them up. She quickly ushered them to the door, and they were outside before Martin could raise a query about the price.

'That's ridiculous; three shillings should get bed and board for a month,' he said to George.

'We have the money, and she needs to get the best care.'

'Best care? I bet they treat her like a dog. Did you see the way that woman sneered at us?' Martin growled back.

Martin and George had never discussed money much, and George would just hand out whatever he thought was appropriate at the end of each month. Martin always told him he was too generous; George, on the other hand, thought he got the best farmhand he could ever buy for the money.

'I'll pay you back when we get home,' Martin said, and George looked somewhat put out.

'I pay for all of our medical costs, and I intend to pay for this.'

Martin began to argue, 'But she isn't...' then thought better of it as he saw the frown George had developed. He nodded and patted his friend on the back as they approached the cart.

Partway home, they encountered another cart, and as they neared, they realised it was Sheffield. The usually haughty and somewhat chic man was on a very plain and unimportant looking vehicle.

They greeted him and then realised the clothes he wore were in poor condition. He did not answer them but nodded.

'Hold up. We need to talk,' George said, and he complied, though he still did not speak. George and Martin got down from their seats and moved to him, standing either side of his cart.

'What has happened, man?' questioned Martin and then literally caught Sheffield as he fell forward and off his seat.

George quickly moved to the same side as Martin and helped to place Sheffield on the ground. It was impossible to miss the powerful stench of alcohol, both stale and fresh.

'He's pickled,' said Martin, and George nodded.

'We're nearer to his farm than to home, so we better take him there.'

The two men needed to say little, as it seemed they read each other's thoughts. They placed their load in the back of his cart and Martin mounted to drive it home. George followed.

Once at the farm, they looked around and could see no one. George moved to the barn, and then to the worker bunkhouse, shouting for assistance, but no one stirred; eventually, he knocked on the door and opened it. As he did, the blast of a shotgun rang out and part of the door was blown away. George dived back into cover and Martin came running with his pistol drawn.

There was silence for a moment, and then George shouted, 'Who's shooting?'

Another stretch of silence passed, and then a shaky voice asked, 'Who's there?'

'It's George Douglas, and why the hell are you shooting?'

An old man poked his head through the doorway and said, 'I'm comin' out.'

He exited, still brandishing the offending gun. Martin quickly took it from him, and he fell to his knees, pleading, 'I didn't mean to. I thought Mr Sheffield had come back – he's been shooting the place up. He's gone mad. The cook and the housekeeper left yesterday, fearing for their own safety.' He took a deep breath, as if he'd forgotten to do so.

'God, you're drunk as well,' said Martin.

'And why wouldn't I be? The man's gone round the bend. They burned his house down, and he's gone lala.' He took another deep breath as Martin helped him up. 'It could've been the blacks coming back to finish us off,' he babbled, and George interrupted him.

'Pull yourself together, man,' he barked, still shaking after the shot nearly took his right ear off.

'I'm sorry, sir,' the old man answered and quickly cringed in fear as George neared.

'Stop carrying on. No one's here to hurt you.'

'Thank you, sir, thank you,' he slurred, bowing twice, though they were very shallow obeisances, as he would've fallen face-first on the ground if he'd gone lower.

'Your boss is in the back of the cart. We'll get him out, and you can look after him,' George said.

'No, no. I won't stay here another bloody minute with that loon,' the man assured him.

'Well, you better get on your horse and get yourself into town,' Martin suggested.

'Would if I could, would if I could, yes, yes, if I could,' he repeated.

George was becoming increasingly annoyed at everything being said twice. Having had an incredibly difficult day already, he shouted at the man, 'Take the damn wagon and get into town! We'll take Sheffield with us. Let his boy know where he is if you can.'

'I will, sir, thank you, I will, I will, but the boy has gone. Had an argument with his father and went off with the rest of the hands. Mad as his father, if you ask me.'

The old man slurred and mumbled as he tried to mount Sheffield's cart. Martin gave him a shove from behind, and they took Sheffield from the buckboard and transferred him to their own cart. He barely stirred. Both men shook their heads and turned for home, the Sheffield wagon in front of them, the horses seemingly knowing the way.

Arriving home, George immediately dismounted and entered the house to tell Sarah the news. She was alone in the kitchen, and he blurted, 'He's dead, Willow's with the doctor and Sheffield's in the back of the cart.'

'Sheffield's dead?'

'No, no, Draper's dead; he fell off a cliff and died. Sheffield has gone a bit crazy and is so drunk he can't stand. We brought him back here because we didn't want him to be alone at his farm. All his workers have gone bush.'

Still looking a bit dumbfounded, Sarah nodded. George exited and helped Martin carry Sheffield into the house; they placed him on the couch and moved to the kitchen to explain things in more depth.

'He fell off a cliff or was pushed?' Sarah raised a quizzical eyebrow.

'There were two troopers there to arrest him. He decided to run and fell off the cliff,' George said, sounding more and more exasperated.

'I'm glad you and Willow had nothing to do with it,' Sarah declared, turning her eyes to Martin.

'We aren't.' He averted his gaze, not wanting to show her the anger and guilt which filled his eyes.

'But you can't mean it,' she continued.

'We needn't talk about that now. It's immaterial. The man is dead.'

George inserted himself into the argument between his wife and best friend, knowing neither would give even a little ground. 'Where are the boys and Carter?'

'Out in the vegetable garden–'

'Martin, could you go and fill them in about Sheffield and Willow? No need to mention Draper's end.'

Martin nodded, though he too would've been ready to continue the argument. Once he left, George continued to Sarah, 'It's no good fighting over this. It's how they both feel, and you'll never change that.'

'And what about you, what do you feel?' she immediately fired back, upset that she should be quieted in her own kitchen.

'I'm not sad that he's dead, but I wouldn't have killed him. Can't we just leave it at that?'

Though it wasn't the answer she craved, she didn't want it to be a barrier between them. Draper had done such terrible things to the children at the orphanage and to her three closest friends. He was dead; she knew she must let it go.

For the next twenty-four hours, Sheffield stayed on the couch being waited on by George and Martin. They found that they needed a bucket for each end when he awoke in the early hours of the morning, and the lounge room had such a terrible odour that the front door was left open. Lavender from the garden was set to burn in the open fireplace.

Late in the afternoon, Sheffield got up from the couch and walked out to the yard, where the boys saw him dry-retching over the garden fence.

'Are you alright, sir?' questioned Sam, and though Sheffield didn't look up, he answered with an open hand, gesturing for them to leave him alone.

The three boys smiled at each other and walked on to the shed. They got the horses ready for night and made sure they had their rations of food and water.

Later in the evening, George entered the lounge to encourage Sheffield to take some food and found him babbling incoherently. George was uncertain if the nonsense he was spouting was due to alcohol poisoning or if he'd simply been unable to cope with the series of unfortunate occurrences which had befallen him.

Speaking to the adults around the table at the end of one of Sarah's beautifully prepared dinners, George stated his intention to summon the doctor if Sheffield's health didn't improve by the next morning.

'Good,' said Martin, who made it obvious he wanted to fetch the doctor to collect Willow, or if not, at least see her.

George and Sarah both nodded without looking at their friend, knowing exactly what he was thinking. Neither begrudged him the opportunity.

The next morning, Sheffield's condition not only didn't improve, but he seemed to become much more confused and incoherent.

Martin rode out shortly. Sarah had insisted that if Willow was to come home, it wouldn't be on the back of a horse. Martin agreed, though he'd said he would ride ahead of the boys, who would be on the cart, to 'prepare things'. George offered to go instead of the boys, but Martin insisted he was needed by Sarah to help look after Sheffield.

'Make sure you all carry your guns,' Sarah said, as the boys moved to the stable to harness the carthorses.

'Yes, Mother,' answered Sam, though there was little doubt the boys would've taken their guns. They knew as well as anyone that in these hard times, there were many people who'd take advantage of unarmed travellers.

Indeed, Sarah's thought seemed to be prophetic, as no sooner than the boys had turned onto the main road, they were confronted by Martin's horse, riderless. James tapped the horses to increase speed, fearing that something terrible had happened. Reaching the animal, they quickly tied it to the cart, and after a short look around, they remounted and brought the horses back to their fast but safe speed.

Sam had drawn his rifle, and he nodded to Leo to do the same. No words were offered. Each knew there was a need to hurry. Martin wasn't a man to just fall from a horse; in fact, on occasion, he'd ridden home from town in a tired and 'under the weather' condition.

Rounding a bend in the road, they could see a group of men. Their horses were in the paddock to the right, and the men were surrounding Martin. Punches had already been thrown. Martin was the worse for wear, having tumbled from his mount when a rope strung between two trees felled it.

The boys quickly dismounted and ran to the bushes on either side of the road. A tall, brutish man threw a punch, which hit Martin in the face. Stumbling backwards, he ran into the ring of men. They all had their faces covered, but the boys could tell that one of the men was Sheffield Junior.

Martin was pushed toward the aggressor again. As the thug prepared to deliver another blow, his momentum was stopped when a bullet smashed through his right leg. He fell to the ground. For a moment, there was little movement from the six other men. Another shot struck the road nearby, and as if they suddenly understood what was happening, the men all dived to the cover of the ditches on either side of the road.

Leo had followed Sam to the right and watched as he fired the two shots. 'I can't shoot anyone,' he said, looking terrified.

'Just fire into the air and make as much noise as you can,' Sam said, feeling sorry for his friend.

Martin had fallen to his knees, only feet away from the wounded man. Now he crawled to the stricken figure and took the pistol from his holster. The man was rolling from side to side, holding his heavily bleeding leg. Martin shielded himself behind the writhing body.

The gang of men were making their way toward the shots.

'It's Douglas. He's only one man,' Sheffield Junior said, looking to drive his men forward.

As the men on the right side began to move, another bullet struck the road and a shot from Leo flew overhead. They all fell back into the gutter, and though the drought was in full bloom, the dip was full of mud. The four men on the left side of the road rose, and one was hit in the arm by a shot from James.

Realising there was no hope with many guns trained on them, the men began to break and run toward their horses. The three on the left side soon gained their steeds, and the three from the right crossed and made it to the fallen tree where the horses had been tied. Several shots rang out around them as they mounted and galloped off.

Moving at a run, James and Sam approached Martin, who stood and limped to meet them. Behind him, the wounded man still writhed on the road.

Suddenly, a shot came from the cart. Leo had stood and fired over the head of his friends, and they all spun to see what he was shooting at. The wounded man lay dead. They turned back to see a dumbfounded Leo standing with the rifle at his shoulder, his mouth agape, as if he couldn't believe what he'd just done. Sam ran to him and slowly took the gun. James hurried to the dead man and found that he'd pulled another hidden weapon and lay with it in his hand.

Martin stood injured and in awe of the three young men who had just saved his life.

As the cart pulled up in front of the doctor's shop, the two brothers sat mounted on the driver's seat. On the back, Martin held the shattered Leo close to him while an unmoving package lay wrapped on his other side.

James ran into the shop to get assistance. Sam tied the horses to the street hitching post and opened the back of the cart to allow the two to get out. Martin couldn't move easily, and Leo wasn't going to let him go, so Sam waited for the doctor.

Arriving, the somewhat put out Doctor West and his belligerent wife quickly took control. He shouted at two men in front of the pub opposite. Soon, they were unloading the stricken Martin and Leo, and then the dead body. All three were carried into the surgery and Martin was laid on a treatment table. Leo was given into the care of the two brothers, and they sat on the floor near Martin's bed. Leo had his head buried in his arms and wept uncontrollably.

The two bystanders took the body into a back room, led by the grumbling old biddy. She delivered them back to the front door and shut it behind them without a word of thanks.

Immediately realising that Martin had broken his right femur, West cut away his pants, not worrying about the remonstrations of his patient. The bone had broken about halfway along its length, and the muscles had contracted. 'You two boys, come here. I'll need your help,' West said, pointing at James and Sam. They quickly obeyed and left Leo with his head still buried.

'I have to set his leg, and you two will need to hold his shoulders,' West barked.

Mrs West, who stood at his right hand, asked, 'What size splint do you need, Doctor?'

'About a ten,' came the answer, then he corrected himself. 'No, no, a twelve, I think.'

'I'll bring both,' she answered and left the room. Returning, she placed the two wooden splints next to the injured leg.

'Hold his shoulders now, and don't let go.' West took Martin's leg in his arms. 'Prepare yourself,' he told Martin, who closed his eyes and gritted his teeth.

West pulled and twisted the leg, and though his patient groaned and the two holding him strained, his grip wasn't loosened until the muscles stretched enough for the bones to meet. Martin groaned even louder, and the two brothers holding him found tears welling up in their eyes as they tried not to look at each other.

West obviously had more strength than his appearance suggested. He held Martin's foot between his knees and positioned the splint by the inside of the leg. Once he was confident he had the correct piece of wood, he packed it and began to bandage it securely so the limb couldn't move. He waved the boys away, and Mrs West attempted to move them from the room, but Leo wouldn't budge from the floor. Eventually, she conceded and left the room, tutting about the young people of today.

Leo remained inconsolable for some minutes, until Martin called for him. 'Boy, you need not cry. You saved my life.'

Leo, who'd obeyed and moved to his side, buried his head in Martin's embrace. 'Enough, now. Stand tall,' Martin ordered, and the boy did as instructed. He backed away from the table a little.

'There will be some questions to answer about the ambush. Say nothing and send them to me,' Martin continued, then a thought came to him. 'Go to Madam Sophie's, tell her what has happened and ask her to come.'

The three boys nodded, and Martin indicated with his head that they should go.

A few minutes later, Sophie bustled along the sidewalk with the boys and, turning the corner of the West Surgery, bumped hard into Captain Allen.

'Pardon me.' Realising the three boys were with her, he added, 'I was just coming to see you all.'

'Well, you can't see us at the moment; we have an injured man to tend to.' Sophie pushed Allen aside and stormed into the doctor's office.

'What do you want, madam?' Mrs West sneered in her usual warm way.

'Get out of the way, Beulah,' Sophie sneered back, with as much pleasantry as she had received.

Entering the treatment room, Sophie, followed by an ever-growing entourage, said, 'I need a minute with your patient, West.'

West, who had been facing away from the door, started, turned, and then decided that the fire in the woman's eye was not to be trifled with. He backed out of the room, being berated by his wife. Allen also left the room, though he wasn't sure why.

'What has happened?' Sophie asked Martin bluntly.

Martin answered, giving a full account of what had transpired on the road. Interjections from James and Sam filled the gaps in his memory, and James completed the story, saying, 'Leo shot the man dead and now we have to answer to the captain.'

'Well, there's nothing wrong with protecting yourself,' she said, with a thoughtful look on her face, and turned to Leo. The boy was red-eyed, and his tears again began to flow. She took him in her arms and held him tightly.

'You need to be happy; you were able to save Mr Martin's life,' she said, giving him a pat on the back.

A few minutes passed with nothing more being said, then a knock on the door brought Sophie to her senses. 'Let me handle this,' she said. Crossing the room, she opened the door. Allen stood waiting.

'I have viewed the body; it's no one I know. I need to find out what happened here,' he muttered.

'Isn't it obvious? These young men were jumped by the gang who've been terrorising everyone passing along the Bathurst Road.'

'Is that right?' Allen asked. 'And who shot the stiff?'

In unison, Sam and Leo said, 'I did.'

Sam then corrected, 'We both did.'

'What?' asked Allen.

'Well, I shot him by accident, and Leo shot him on purpose,' Sam answered.

'What?' the man repeated, in an even more incredulous voice.

'They were fighting on the road, and I shot to stop them and accidently hit the man in the leg,' Sam blurted.

After a few seconds of thought, Allen asked, 'Who were you fighting in the road and why?'

'I was riding ahead, and my horse was tripped by a rope stretched across the road... It was that bunch of trouble who've been hanging around with Sheffield Junior,' Martin answered. 'The boys fired lots of shots, and the cowards took to their heels.'

Seeing the puzzled look on Allen's face, he continued, 'The dead man was still lying on the ground as Sam and James rode up, and when Leo brought up the cart, the animal pulled another gun. He was about to shoot me in the back, so Leo shot him.'

Martin was babbling, explaining himself as clearly as he could. Slowly comprehending, Allen turned to Leo and asked, 'That true, boy?'

Leo nodded, looking at the floor.

'Well, as there are no other voices to be heard at this time, it seems I can do nothing but believe you,' Allen concluded.

'Of course you believe them. They were attacked,' Sophie said scornfully.

'There are things we have to do when there's an unlawful killing,' he answered, becoming a little annoyed at her interference.

'You're just upsetting the boy for no good reason,' she said, holding Leo's head to her again as tears flowed down his cheeks.

'We can't have people shooting each other willy-nilly. The boy needs to answer for himself,' Allen added.

'They have answered your questions,' Sophie said stridently.

'That will do for now, but there may be further questions if someone comes forward with extra information.' Allen turned to leave.

'The Douglas farm is at risk with us not there, and that bunch of bastards know it,' Martin blurted.

'Yes, I'll take some men and go out that way,' Allen answered.

Martin sat up with some difficulty, as if he were going to join him.

'I don't need your help,' Allen assured him.

'Yes, but we were coming to get the doctor. Old Sheffield has lost his marbles and is being looked after by the Douglas clan.'

'I'll take the doctor with me.'

'And the boys,' Martin insisted and received a nod of agreement.

Chapter 15

AT THE FARM, George stood looking out the front door, wondering why it was taking so long to return with the doctor. Sarah sat at Sheffield's side, mopping his brow with a damp cloth. Carter was in the kitchen preparing a pot of tea at her request.

'If I can get some hot tea into him, it may help,' she reasoned.

George turned to meet her gaze, and she shook her head. He stepped back and went to shut the door when a shot rang out. The bullet smashed into the frame to his right. Splinters peppered his face and flew into the room.

George shut the door and slammed the bolts home, then grabbed for his gun, which was sitting as usual near the entrance. Pulling a large splinter from his bleeding cheek, he was joined by Carter with his rifle. Sarah was quickly on her feet and moved to the kitchen to gather her shotgun.

'Keep down, everyone; I can only see one man,' George warned, as he looked through the viewing slot in the door.

'What the hell is going on?' Carter exclaimed, throwing himself on the floor near the small window at the side of the room.

'The back door,' Sarah exclaimed. Rushing into the kitchen, she slammed the wooden strut support across the door, then moved to the window and pushed the shutter closed, locking it. As she backed away, a shot shattered the timber and lodged in her shoulder. She let out a cry of pain and hit the ground hard. George knew from the sound that she'd been struck. He ran with head down as several more bullets crashed through the front door, and he came to her side. Realising how much blood he saw, he grabbed for the tablecloth, rolled it into a bundle and placed it over the wound.

Before he could move further, he heard the front door locks being slid back, and the door opened. He dashed back to the front room. Sheffield had gained his feet and, seeing Sarah's shotgun on the floor, had gathered it and stumbled out the door. As he exited the veranda, a bullet ripped into his abdomen.

A shout of 'Stop!' came from outside the house. A figure ran to the fallen man, but on his arrival, he was met by the retort of Sheffield's weapon. He fell dead. Thinking better of their position, the other offending men gathered horses from behind the barn, mounted, and rode away as quickly as they were able. Two men at the rear of the house heard the other horses galloping off and began to move to join their cronies.

As the two arrived at the front gates of the property, they were confronted by Captain Allen, six of his men and the cart with West and the three boys on board. They threw up their arms when challenged and were placed under arrest by two of the troopers. The rest of the party rushed to the house.

Sheffield lay next to the body in the front yard. West swiftly dismounted and rushed to the two stricken bodies. Seeing Sheffield's wound, he called, 'Get me cloth and water.'

Allen nodded to his men, and they bolted in the direction of the house to comply.

George had returned to Sarah and assured her that everything was going to be alright, in the way one does when there is little conviction in the statement. He continued to put pressure on her wound and, as the first trooper entered the room, called for help. The second trooper entered, grabbed a blanket from the nearest bedroom and ran back to the doctor.

'The woman has been shot, sir,' he said to his commanding officer, as he passed the blanket to West. Grabbing it, West bundled it into Sheffield's abdomen to stem the bleeding. He then stood and ran to the house to treat Sarah.

Quickly assessing the woman's condition, he asked for her to be placed on the kitchen table. He called for his bag and, with the dexterity of a much younger man, began to remove fragments of the bullet from her body.

'Bring the man in. He'll need surgery next,' West ordered.

Allen stood over the two bodies in the courtyard and, for a moment, said and did nothing.

Sheffield had moved only a little as he turned himself to be in closer proximity to the other body. Reaching over, he removed the hood from his victim and stared into the eyes of his son.

He let out a bloodcurdling scream of anguish and lapsed into unconsciousness.

The three boys entered the kitchen with Carter, who had injured himself while diving to his defensive position. He limped, supported by Leo.

West fastened the last of the stitches in Sarah's wound. Stoic as ever, she looked up at them reassuringly. 'What has happened to you?' she asked.

Sam and James explained as they lifted and carried her to her bed, where they lay with her. The troopers, under directions from the surgeon, brought his next case to him.

Sheffield was wan and still unconscious. Stripped to his waist, his wound was disinfected with pouring brandy, and an incision was made below it. Immediately, gushing blood was soaked up by the cloth, and another was placed into the wound to clear it, allowing West to see the damage.

When he had done his initial assessment, he looked at Allen and George, who stood together at the end of the table, and shook his head to indicate that there was little he could do for Sheffield.

'The man he brought down was his son,' Allen said, not looking at anyone in particular.

'Oh, God,' George exclaimed.

West added, 'Best if he doesn't wake at all, then,' and though he thought it was probably pointless, he continued to operate.

Later, as he left with the captain, troopers, prisoners, and two bodies, West said to George, 'I don't think he'll live, but if he gets to the end of the week, I'll come back and see how the wound is.'

The other two attackers had disappeared into the bush from the back of the house, pursued by two troopers.

Two days passed with Sheffield near death. During her convalescence, Sarah was cared for by the three boys, who waited on her hand and foot. She continually protested the attention, but secretly adored the wonderful young men they were becoming. Sheffield's condition continued without any real change, and though West had not come back to see him, he seemed to be faring no worse.

The family stayed inside the house most of the time, only venturing outside when there were chores to complete. Carter had taken to sitting for long periods in the 'crow's nest', as he termed the roof-mounted hide. There, he leant his back against the stone chimney and whittled. He came down only when relieved by Leo, thinking he was doing the only constructive thing he could under the circumstances. If there was another attack, he would be ready and waiting, or Leo would.

There were no other raids. Indeed, for another three days, no one visited the farm at all.

After church on the Sunday, West arrived, bringing Martin and Willow home. He was most surprised to see Sheffield still alive. Even more surprising was the fact that the man had eaten some soup prepared for him in the last two days.

Taking the covering off the wound, West could see that despite being serious and inflamed, it was showing signs of closing up. He hadn't stitched the edges together, having decided not to attempt to remove the bullet. He'd seen no good reason to put him through the extra trauma of opening the area further.

Re-bandaging the wound, he said to George, 'I didn't think he would live, but there seems to be no infection and he is breathing fairly normally.'

The two men nodded, and Carter said, 'I couldn't understand what he was saying, but he even spoke a few words this morning.'

'Look, if there were any chance of me getting him into town alive, I would put him on the cart, but he just wouldn't make it,' West said apologetically.

'No need to worry, doc. The boys, Carter and I are running our own little hospital anyhow,' George said, looking over at the lounge chair, where Martin was sitting with Willow standing beside him.

West stood, nodding, then headed for the door. 'I'll need to change all of their dressings tomorrow. In the meantime, if you need me, send someone.'

'Thanks,' George said, as Carter escorted West to his cart.

George got up, moved to Willow, and gave her a hug. Neither of them issued a word, but Martin, relaxing back into his chair, said, 'She's already taken, man.'

Willow gave him a playful backhanded slap, and then looked aghast as he held his wounded shoulder as if in pain. He looked up at her and laughed. She slapped him again, and the three all beamed at each other.

Willow was back. The real Willow.

Later in the afternoon, Sheffield awoke and even sat up for a few minutes. He didn't speak but nodded to indicate he understood what was being said to him. Sarah, too, had got out of bed for a short time and sat in the lounge chair with the three boys clustered around her.

Willow had assumed the role of cook from Carter and was baking and roasting an amazing number of dishes on and in the wood-fired stove. 'Everyone wash up for dinner. It'll be served in about fifteen minutes,' she announced.

The family all gathered at the table, except Sarah, who, feeling a little sore, had returned to her bed. Sheffield remained on the couch, sleeping.

Willow placed the many dishes in front of the ravenous crowd: potatoes in their jackets and mashed in huge bowls; beans, pumpkin, corn; a large container of steak and kidney steaming in the middle. A foot-long beef Wellington and two plates of boiled eggs rounded off the repast.

Carter said grace, and Willow prepared a small plate of food, which she took to Sarah. They sat quietly as Sarah ate, and they continually glanced at each other, lost for words. Finally, Sarah broke the silence.

'I'm so glad you're back,' she said sincerely, then added, 'though with food like this, I may lose my job.'

'No chance, but I would love to help you in the kitchen,' Willow replied, with an expectant gleam in her eyes.

She took the plate as Sarah finished and returned to the kitchen, where the larger portion of the food she'd prepared had been consumed.

'Wonderful meal,' Martin complimented her, and the entire group, huddled around the table, echoed his words.

'Apple pie to finish?' Willow beamed, delighted at the response, and heads nodded in agreement.

The meal completed, Willow moved to the lounge and offered Sheffield a small meal. Though he tried to refuse, she sat and began to spoon-feed him.

Chapter 16

THREE WEEKS PASSED, and though there had been sightings of the Wiradjuri outlaws, no further attacks had occurred. The troopers, led by Captain Allen, had continually gone out looking but had never picked up a trail.

The Pembury farm was then attacked by the Wiradjuri troop, with John Pembury killed and his wife and two daughters left without a breadwinner. It was suspected by many that Pembury was one of the unnamed members of Sheffield Junior's band.

The Wiradjuri did not suspect; they knew.

George had driven to town to buy some basic supplies. He was surprised to see a large gathering outside the Elephant and Castle Hotel on George Street. Mayor Harley Williams was again being lambasted about the situation.

'What the hell are you doing about it?' one man called out.

Before Williams could answer, another had added, 'Bloody nothing, he always does nothing!'

'I'll thank you to keep a civil tongue in your mouth, Bill Thompson,' Williams blurted, and as the shouting died down, he continued. 'The captain has assured me there will be a party on their heels this very afternoon. He's got in two black trackers, as his men haven't been able to find the troop.'

The gathering paused, as if to take in this new information, then Thompson shouted, 'How safe are the outlying farms?'

Williams again raised his voice to be heard over the vociferous mob. 'We are doing everything we can.'

'What are you doing for the Pembury Family?' another person asked, and though the voice sounded to George that of a woman, he could not see where it came from.

'The family have been brought into town and are being looked after by friends.' Williams paused for effect. 'We are going to hunt these animals down and deal with them.'

This statement was met with some applause and some doubtful moans. George shook his head and entered the store, where he purchased flour, sugar, tea and tobacco.

'Taken to smoking, then?' questioned the storeowner.

'No, it's for Sheffield.'

'He's well enough to smoke, then?'

'Not really, but he is insistent,' George answered, thinking that it wasn't the inquisitive man's business.

'Well, he'll soon be up and around, then?' asked the man, who seemed to have a strange speech impediment which dictated that he end every sentence with the word 'then'.

George shrugged his shoulders and, receiving his change, headed for the door.

'Give him my best, then. Damn good customer, you know, Douglas?'

The man seemed fit to continue, but George had exited.

The crowd who'd been grilling the mayor had dwindled, and now a few stood with him on the covered walkway at the front of the hotel. George noticed Allen approaching with two trackers and eight soldiers, mounted in double file.

The few people on the street began to clap. Allen dipped his hat to Williams and continued past. George looked long and hard at the two trackers. How must they feel being given the job of tracking down their own kind?

Little did he know they'd been given no chance to opt out of the position. Indeed, they had been taken from the stockades and told what they were going to do. Both had refused. Their family members were threatened, and they were told they would be hanged as collaborators if they didn't find Jaiemba's troop within a week.

Allen saw this as the only way he could be sure of finding the devils terrorising his area. He certainly didn't take any notice of those, like George, who thought they had good reason for what they were doing. George didn't support the killing, but he did understand why they were enraged to the point of madness. Their families were wantonly slaughtered, and no one was helping *them* get justice.

Allen nodded at George as he passed, and George nodded back, not having anything else in his mind to do.

The trackers took the lead when the group reached the Sheffield farm and headed to the station at Napoleon Reef. They looked all the time at the ground and bushes, noticing everything from footprints to broken branches. An hour's good ride past the Reef, they found the remains of a fire and nodded to Allen.

'How long?' he asked.

One of the men answered, 'Maybe two weeks.'

'Keep going. We still have a couple hours before dark,' Allen ordered, and the group moved off to the north at a relatively slow pace.

At night, they camped in a clearing at the far west of the Sheffield property, near the massacre site. They didn't go quite far enough to find the dam, but the next morning, they came upon it only minutes after breaking camp.

The poison bottles were still lying around the edge of the hole, but no bodies were present. Jaiemba and his troop had returned and taken the fallen. No one knew where.

The trackers rode through, not looking back at the site until they were some distance away. Allen simply shook his head, and the troop continued.

The rest of the morning was lost to a fruitless detour to Pembury Farm. The trackers searched for signs of the Wiradjuri troop but found none. Allen cursed at and threatened them in very poor Wiradjuri, and one of them replied in almost-as-poor English. 'Them like ghosts, boss.'

'Rubbish. Your time is running out, so you better find them,' Allen ordered in English and then swore again in their native tongue.

The two men looked at each other, made a few indistinct signs with their hands, and turned their horses back to the east. At the next cutting between hills, they turned again, toward Sofala.

Within an hour, they had reached the main street of the little village. Locals came out of the hotel and shop to see the passing parade, and though Allen knew several of the inhabitants, he only nodded and rode on, following his trackers. Several small children ran along the rough footpath, watching the soldiers and pretending to shoot them with imaginary pistols.

At the corner next to the pub, two women and a man who appeared to Allen to have some 'coloured blood' walked to the edge of the road and spat at the trackers. The two men did not react, choosing to look away, and those making the assault said several unsavoury things in a broken tongue which the soldiers did not recognise. One of the women then shouted 'Traitors!' and other English words which would have been less surprising if they'd come from the mouth of a sailor.

'Back away!' Allen ordered and pulled his side arm.

The man obeyed, but the two women stood irresolute and unflinching. Allen thought better of his actions and returned his weapon to its holster. He positioned his horse in front of the two women and said, less forcefully, 'Get off the road, or I will have you arrested'. They ignored him but were moved when the horse's flank brushed in front of them as the parade continued out of town.

Late in the afternoon, they passed onto the Brucedale property and were seen by the three boys, who were driving a few head of wayward sheep back to the main paddock. Allen raised his arm and was answered by the boys in turn. They were never in verbal contact, as the boys went about their business and the group passed on toward the Bathurst road.

Jaiemba and his men had skirted around Bathurst to the south. A cold wind had sprung from the west, and though bitter to the European migrants, the Wiradjuri warriors travelled quickly and with little clothing to warm them. They knew these conditions, as their forbears had for thousands of years, and knew that the best thing to do was keep moving.

They were headed for the newly established town of Blayney, a small settlement in the valley of the Belubula River – then known as King's Plains. Jaiemba knew they would find one of the men who'd taken part in the massacre at the Sheffield waterhole there.

Jack Poole had joined Sheffield Junior's gang when his final dam had dried up for the third year in succession. His family were potentially going to starve, as they had no access to banks or moneylenders like Sheffield Senior, who would hire men for a pittance in hard times, aware they would have to work for whatever wage was offered. Poole hated the Sheffields and knew they would take his land if they wanted to extend their holdings into the Blayney-Cowra area.

The massacre had been completed by a few of the gang's members under the direction of Sheffield Junior. Though Poole hadn't been present at the beginning of the event, he'd arrived when the poison had been laid.

The Wiradjuri troop didn't know this fact, but he'd been seen with the gang, and they were going to take revenge on as many as they could. Poole had heard about the killing of Pembury and knew he would be next on the list. He was quickly preparing to move everything he owned into the town; he stood hitching the cart to its horse, glancing furtively in all directions. All the furniture, though poor in quality, had been loaded, and now smaller, more delicate items were placed where they wouldn't be crushed. He had explained to his wife and two daughters, who were ten and twelve, that there would be time to sell the land when they reached the safety of the town.

Dragging the large but light bathtub, he again returned to the side of the cart and began to manoeuvre it into lifting position. Bending down, he heaved it to the top of the load and was caught in the grasp of one of Jaiemba's men as he stepped backwards to admire his work.

He let out a whimper, like the cowering cur he was, and fell to his knees. The man stood over him with spear raised, waiting for his leader to give the order.

Jenny Poole had heard the noise from inside the house and, looking through the window, realised her worst fears. She rushed to the shotgun, which was kept behind the front door. As the man raised the spear to strike, he was hit heavily in the chest. The gun's retort pushed Jenny back slightly from the front door.

Her aim was true, and he fell dead.

Before Jaiemba could react, one of his warriors had hurled a spear, which buried itself in Jenny's chest. She was propelled backwards even further into the room, knocking the paraffin lantern over in her fall. The entire incident had taken but a few seconds, and now the house was alight.

The eldest girl appeared at the door. Seeing her father kneeling, now under the weapon of another man, and having witnessed her mother fall, she turned slowly away from the scene and moved back into the burning room.

Jaiemba, not wishing to harm the children, reached out his hand and moved to bring her from the flames. Seeing him but not believing that there was another choice, she closed the door. The sliding of the bolt was audible as it sealed her, her sister and her mother's body inside the inferno.

Poole let out a bloodcurdling scream as all that he held so dear was taken by the fire. Then, as miraculously as they had appeared, the troop, even the fallen man, was gone.

Struggling to his feet, Poole ran to the door, which was fully engulfed in flames. He grabbed at the handle, and its impression was burned into the flesh of his hand. He was beaten back by the flames. In vain, he ran to the well, drawing a bucket of what was almost entirely mud, and returned to the now fully engulfed façade. He delivered the pitiful contents. It did nothing, and he returned to the well and drew an even thicker sludge. This too had no real effect on the flames. Now he stumbled to the animal trough in the barn, but that too was dry.

Earlier in the day, the three cows had been milked. He dragged the milk urn to the front veranda and poured it, as best he could, over the ever-growing flames. This allowed him to get close enough to kick the door in, though as it opened, the inner roof collapsed, and the flames beat him back again.

He had been fighting with no chance, and now realised that his family were gone.

Falling to his knees once more, he let out a terrible cry, and wished that the Wiradjuri had killed him before he had seen the awful carnage.

The next morning, Poole sat in almost the same position when Allen and his men rode up. Quickly dismounting, the troopers formed a perimeter, and Allen moved to the stricken man and tried to lift him from the cold soil.

'Where is your...' he began to ask but stopped when he saw Poole's distraught and bewildered face.

He could also see the smouldering remains of the house.

The faithful old carthorse had stayed in position near the barn and stood hitched and ready for the task ahead. Allen eventually dragged the shell of Poole to the cart and had him loaded, then ordered one of his men, 'Take the poor bastard back into town.'

Poole didn't immediately realise what was happening, being stupefied by the previous evening's events. When he did, he became enraged and demanded to go with the force to kill the Wiradjuri troop.

Allen said simply, 'No, you must go back into Bathurst.'

Poole began to argue loudly and in an almost incoherent voice. 'I will come, I will, I will.'

Allen eventually made out what he was saying. 'No. You should go to town, where you'll be safe,' he said, feeling the man's obvious distress.

More babbling came from Poole. He threw himself from the cart, and then, struggling, he got to his feet and began to unhitch the horse.

Allen hesitated and then said to his men, 'This is the closest we've got to these animals. We'll have to leave him.' He remounted and signalled for the trackers to move out.

'Stay here, man,' he said to Poole, turned with his troopers, and followed the two Wiradjuri men, who read the prints in the dust with ease.

They left the frantic Poole trying to find a saddle for the horse and knew he would most likely follow them. And follow them he did, staying around five hundred yards to the rear of the last trooper.

By midday, Sergeant Gayner, second in charge to Allen, could bear it no longer and pulled his horse alongside his leader.

'Sir, he is still following us,' he commented.

'I have eyes in my head, Sergeant,' Allen said and looked back over his shoulder to see Poole, who was being watched by the entire group.

He turned his horse and signalled a halt. Poole, too, stopped.

Thinking better of his earlier decision to leave him, Allen motioned to several of the men to go back. 'Bring him up,' he ordered.

Poole was brought to Allen's side, and the group turned and rode off with no words passing between them, bar an instruction from Allen.

'You do as I say.'

Poole nodded his agreement, and the party again fell in line with the trackers.

Chapter 17

SHEFFIELD'S CONDITION HAD become stable, and he joined the family for the first time at the table for luncheon. His head remained bowed most of the time, and he avoided making eye contact with anyone. He felt guilt, remorse, and horror at the son he had brought into the world and accidentally removed from it. He knew the boy had missed his mother from an early age after her death, and his own aloofness had been the catalyst for the boy's rebellious behaviour.

The meal was eaten in a much quieter room than usual, the group living under the pall of what had happened to this once proud and haughty man. Leo broke the silence in his usual awkward way, saying, 'I wonder if they've got Jaiemba?'

He received no answer, but a stern look from Carter told him to shut up as if the man had spoken the very words.

After all plates were removed from the table, Sheffield asked George if he could be taken into the town in the afternoon. Sarah interrupted, saying, 'You aren't well enough to travel yet,' as she frowned at the man, genuinely caring about his health.

'I have to go sometime, and... I need to put the farm in order and look after my crew,' he answered, alluding to his six or seven workers, who were still in his employ.

'Are you sure you're well enough?' returned George. Though he still hadn't grown to like Sheffield, he did pity his plight.

'I'll take a room in the hotel for a few days, and I can have West come and see me and get Solicitor White to rewrite my will. I'll also need to appoint someone to look after the farm for a while.'

Silence gripped the room again for a short time, until George said, 'You know you're welcome here if you want to stay, but if you want to go, I'll drive you in on the cart.'

Sheffield lifted his gaze. 'Thank you, but I must get on,' he said. True gratitude showed in his expression for just a moment, and then his eyes became lifeless again and dropped from his host.

In little more than an hour, the cart was readied. With Sheffield loaded on the back in a makeshift seat, constructed by the boys from a couple of bales of hay, blankets and a pillow, the two left for Bathurst. Surprisingly, clouds began to fill the sky, and by the time they reached the Bathurst road, there was a slight drizzle floating almost horizontally into George's face. He tapped the horses to bring them to a trot. Sheffield dragged one of the blankets from beneath himself and covered his already wet head as the horses moved at a faster pace.

George, looking around at his passenger, asked, 'Will you be OK?' and Sheffield nodded his shrouded head.

By the time they arrived outside Doctor West's surgery, they were both soaking wet. George tied the horses to the rail, and then, taking Sheffield's arm, he assisted the older man to the entrance.

Mrs West answered the door and said, in much more pleasant tones than George was used to, 'Oh, Mr Sheffield. Oh, oh, you poor man.'

She cleared a path for the men to enter, giving George a withering glare. This was the Mrs West he knew.

'What is the meaning of bringing this poor man here in this condition?' she demanded.

'It was dry when we left home,' George answered, in the voice of a defendant.

'Calm down, woman. He did as I demanded,' Sheffield said impatiently.

'Oh, yes, sir,' she answered, still glaring in George's direction.

'Where's West?' Sheffield said.

'He's up at the Elephant,' she answered, alluding to the hotel.

'Well, get him here.'

Mrs West rushed out of the room. In around fifteen minutes, West was led in and presented to Sheffield. His wife then bustled George back to the front door.

As he was about to depart, she said, 'We'll look after him from here,' and promptly slammed the door, almost hitting him. Just as he'd come to expect of this woman. She seemed to think her importance was above mere mortals'.

George had wanted to say he would return to see if Sheffield needed assistance, but Mrs West's rudeness made him unsure what to do next. He mounted his horse and trotted the hundred yards to the hotel. On entering, he found Sheffield's bunkhouse cook sitting at the end of the bar; he appeared to be in a heavily inebriated condition.

George stood before him, and after a short time, the man realised George was looking to address him.

'What do you want?' he blurted and took a swig of whatever concoction he'd ordered.

'Sheffield's at the doctor's, and it looks like he'll recover OK from the shooting. He'll need his staff. Especially now there's rain.'

'Go back there? I don't bloody think so.' The man snorted and guzzled another drink. 'He took pot shots at us last time we were there, and he shot his own son. Not bloody likely.'

'He was very drunk and ill, and he didn't know it was his son,' George corrected. 'He needs you to get his foreman to come and see him. He's coming here for further recovery. You'd better not be drunk when he arrives, as he might deal with you.'

'I'm not scared of him anymore,' the drunkard skited, almost spitting with every word.

'Well, I could go and tell him that if you like, or I could tell him you're looking for the foreman.'

The man took almost a minute to process the statement and then thought better of his next action. Sheffield had been his cash cow for nearly twenty years, and he had no other real prospects. He stood and took the last tipple from his glass, saying, 'I'll get Stone to come here later today, but only because I feel sorry for the poor old fool.'

George ordered a beer. He wasn't a drinker, having seen what it had done to his father and many others back in England, but on this occasion, he knew he could be waiting for quite a while and decided one beer wouldn't do any harm. Taking the glass after paying, he moved to a table at the back of the room and sat watching the world pass by. *The beer's a very poor drop*, George thought and sat minding the glass for almost an hour.

At the end of that time, Al Stone entered and addressed the bartender. 'Is Sheffield here yet?'

George stood and moved to Stone as the bartender shook his head. 'I brought him in. He's with Dr West,' George informed Stone.

'And he asked for me?' he questioned further.

'Yes, he isn't particularly well, but I think he needs to get the farm back up and running,' George answered as they left the bar together.

At the surgery, they were greeted by Mrs West. For once, she was civil and invited them in.

'The doctor will be with you shortly,' she said. 'Perhaps you would like tea while you're waiting?' She looked expectantly at George with the thin veneer of a smile.

'No, thank you,' he answered, not knowing what to make of this new friendliness.

'Suit yourselves, then,' she said and left the room.

Soon after, one of the two White brothers, Adam or Graeme – George was never sure which was which – exited the treatment room, dipped his hat and left. West appeared at the door and beckoned the two men to Sheffield's side.

'Boss,' Stone said and nodded.

Sheffield nodded back and then said to George, 'Thank you, Douglas. I will repay you one day.'

'No need,' George said and left the room, understanding that he had been dismissed.

Mrs West appeared and opened the door, bowing almost double. George was surprised and mused that she must've thought he'd been given a peerage or knighted in the last couple of hours.

During this trip to town, George was told by several friends that there had been two other mass killings in the area. The vigilantes had ridden into one camp and just opened fire. All of the Wiradjuri were said to have been killed. He felt so distraught; these people were not even involved in earlier events. The other massacre was much less clear. Somebody said that somebody said that many Wiradjuri were killed, their bodies mutilated. George knew that there would be some truth in the tale but could learn no more.

Back at the farm, a deluge had fallen. Though there was rain all the way home, George gave thanks for the bounty. It would give life to the crops, and the cattle and sheep would begin to reproduce quickly. He smiled as he rode the cart through the front gates of Brucedale and noticed immediately that the first of the dams was already full.

Going straight to the barn, he unhitched the horses and put them in their stalls before stripping his muddied pants and drenched coat. Wrapping a horse blanket around himself and covering his head, he ran across the courtyard to the front door.

Entering, he was greeted by Sarah with a towel and clean, dry clothes. He went directly to the bedroom and changed, shivering as he did. Though it was only autumn, there was a bitterness in the wind, and it gripped him now even more than it had on the trail.

Sarah had food and hot tea ready for him, and he ate as the family watched on. They had earlier eaten a baked lamb dinner, and all sat around the kitchen fire, keeping out of the weather and keeping warm.

The rain lasted for more than two days. By the time the sun came out again, everyone was content with the amount of water, which had seen all the dams in the area filled to overflowing.

Chapter 18

JAIEMBA AND THREE of his men trudged through the rain, moving along the edge of the Wiradjuri-named Belubula River. This was a rich area, and much bush food could be found along the shores. The Wiradjuri name had the meant 'Big Lagoon', or 'Stony River'; no one had ever been sure which.

The men had moved further inland after the burning of the homestead at Blayney, knowing they would now be hunted ever more tenaciously. Their lust for revenge had not been sated, but they hadn't intended to kill the woman and children and were saddened that the events had taken the turn they did.

The other three members of the troop had earlier in the day looped away from the river and come back onto its shores further downstream, hoping to trap one of the mobs of kangaroos between the two groups. They would only fell one of the bigger animals, as they needed only to eat for that day and never wasted meat.

As Jaiemba's group approached a large waterhole on the bend of the river, one of the men stopped and signalled to the others, indicating that he'd heard something unexpected. They all stood like statues and waited. After a short time, they released the pose, satisfied there was nothing to worry about.

The rain fell heavily, and the ground was muddy. They crept closer to the waterhole, hoping to find a group of kangaroos sheltering under the massive old eucalypts, which were almost equidistant, as if once planted along the Belubula.

As they reached a clearing, the wary men paused again and stood watching and listening. Moments passed. Suddenly, a shot rang out, and the first warrior fell as a projectile smashed into his chest. The three others began to scatter but found themselves surrounded. The crossfire came from the bush and from behind the very trees they were approaching. As yet, they had not seen the attackers, so no spears were thrown. Another fell, and Jaiemba ran toward the water with the other following. They'd been ambushed, and the water offered their only chance of salvation.

Jaiemba was dropped by another shot from the opposite side of the river and fell facedown in the water. The last man, seeing one of the trackers, stepped from the cover of a tree, readied his spear and let fly. It killed the man as he stood, and then the last Wiradjuri man fell, Allen firing the final shot.

Coming out from their hiding places, the troopers approached the fallen. Poole, who'd fired one of the first shots of the confrontation, fell on the nearest warrior, stabbing him in the back with a large knife.

'Enough!' ordered Allen, but there was no change in Poole's action. Allen moved toward him and again shouted for him to stop. Again, he was not heeded. He and Gayner had to bodily drag Poole from the corpse.

Poole swung around as if to attack, but Gayner was too fast and had taken his knife before he had the chance to do any more damage. Poole's eyes were inflamed with a hatred which would not easily be quelled.

'Get a hold of yourself, man!' Allen shouted and slapped Poole across the face. Poole fell. Gayner knelt beside him and quickly tied his hands together with a strap from his belt. Poole struggled, but being facedown, was not about to get up easily.

'Stay there!' Allen yelled and then moved toward the next fallen. As he reached the shattered man, he was struck in the back by a spear from across the clearing. The weapon, flying from side-on, did not imbed itself but glanced off. Allen fell, though not fatally wounded.

The other three Wiradjuri, who weren't with the group ambushed, had come up. Another of the soldiers was wounded, a spear imbedding in his shoulder. Gayner took control and, falling to the ground, covered Allen from further assault. All the other soldiers followed his lead and dropped to the ground, several behind tree trunks, and returned fire.

The youngest of the Wiradjuri, a boy of about sixteen, was hit in the chest and fell. Another spear came hurtling through the air in the direction of Gayner, missing narrowly, and imbedded in a tree at his back.

Poole struggled to his feet and stumbled toward Gayner, before being struck down by a rock. The last two warriors had hurled their spears and now resorted to using whatever they could pick up as weapons.

Almost simultaneously, bullets hit them both, and they fell. One, however, got back up and threw another rock before collapsing again. Gayner, seeing the last warrior drop, called, 'Cease fire!'

The clearing was silent. No one moved, everyone listening.

Soon, it was decided that the last of the Wiradjuri were on the ground. The soldiers moved from their places of hiding and went to inspect their victims. The three who'd come into the fight late lay within three yards of each other. The young, unbearded man was still alive, the others dead.

Allen had regained his equilibrium and moved into a sitting position. He looked on as Gayner raised his rifle and shot the young man. To put him out of his misery, as he later claimed.

Gayner returned to his fallen leader and called for one of the men to bring bandages. The wound on Allen's back was deep. The spear had glanced off his spine and left a bloody, gaping gash of about eight or nine inches, through which the back of his ribcage was clearly visible.

As the wound was treated, one of the soldiers called out, 'He's gone?'

Gayner stood and moved to the edge of the river, beside his junior. Where Jaiemba's body had fallen, there were only drag marks. Drag marks that led to the river.

The soldiers ran up and down the edges of the water, scouring its breadth. Nothing could be seen of the badly wounded man.

As Gayner began to formulate a plan of action to continue the search, another soldier shouted that the second tracker was also gone.

'They must've gone down the river. Search in pairs on each side,' he yelled, pointing at the nearest four of his men. The rest of the soldiers were treating their fallen comrades, and one turned Poole to reveal that he was dead.

All of the wounded were moved next to Allen, who was spitting orders and fighting to stand.

'Stay, sir. You're bleeding too heavily to move,' the soldier treating him said, and helped lower him back to the ground.

Suddenly, the troop's horses galloped through the camp from the hiding place near some rocks. They were panicked and running madly. A soldier stood and tried to stop one, only to be knocked to the ground. The horses continued their manic flight and, without halting, plunged through the river and bolted away on the flatter side. Several soldiers followed in an attempt to bring them to heel, but soon all were out of view.

Several hours were spent searching the river for Jaiemba and the missing tracker, but they were never found.

The horses eventually gathered in a clearing, eating grass as if nothing had happened, and they were collected easily and returned to the troop. A litter was made to carry Allen. Although this took some time, they were on the road to Blayney before nightfall. The other wounded troopers were helped to their mounts, and the fallen soldiers were strapped to their horses and led in procession. The bodies of the Wiradjuri were left, like their kin, lying where they were killed on the sands of time.

The troop were now without trackers; however, there was little difficulty in finding the path which passed for a road to Blayney. Around eight o'clock that night, the bedraggled group reached the nearest Blayney homestead and took up residence in the large barn after they turned the farmer's horses out of their shelter.

Allen was taken into the house. The kindly woman who'd managed the farm since her husband's death earlier in the year redressed his wounds with great skill and gave him several hot drinks. After an hour or so, she added broth to the menu, forcing him to take small sips, even though he assured her he didn't need food.

The wound on his back was open, and bone was still visible. The woman moved to the barn to discuss his condition with Gayner.

'You know he is in great danger of the wound getting infected if it isn't closed?' she said. 'I think you should send for a doctor.'

'Yes, ma'am. I'll send someone in the morning,' he answered and began to turn as if moving back to the shed.

'No! That isn't good enough,' she blurted.

Turning back toward her, he asked, 'Do you think it's that bad?'

'Yes, it is close to the spine, and he'll have a difficult time healing... I am no doctor.'

'I'll send a man now, then,' he conceded and walked back into the shed, which was now strewn with the resting bodies of the soldiers. 'I need a volunteer to go to Bathurst, now. The cap's in a bad way.'

No one had initially got up or even raised their hand, but on hearing that their much-loved leader was in a bad condition, several hands went up. One young man jumped to his feet.

'You, Billings?' his superior questioned.

'Yes, sir,' the lad quickly answered.

'Well done, then.'

Once mounted, Billings headed off toward Bathurst. It was a very dark and threatening night. The rain had lingered around the hills, but as he reached the crossing of the Belubula, it again began to pour. He gave his mount a couple of kicks in the ribs to encourage her to quicken. She obeyed.

The sun had risen to a cloudy and wet morning as the young soldier rode into Bathurst's main thoroughfare. There were no people on the streets, though a light still shone in the front bar of the Elephant and Castle.

Billings walked his mount slowly to Dr West's surgery and rapped on the door. Several minutes passed, and there was no reply, so he knocked again, even louder. After another minute or so, Mrs West answered the door, pulling it open and glaring at the young man as she said, 'What time of day do you think it is? You would wake the dead, banging on the door like a lunatic.' She didn't allow him to answer, continuing, 'Respectable people would be in bed. You'd better have good reason–'

Billings stammered as he interrupted her. 'S-S-Sorry, Mrs West, but the captain has been badly wounded and needs the doctor now.'

She didn't answer him but bustled away to fetch her husband.

Moments later, she came back to the door and said, 'He's not here.'

Billings thought, *They must sleep in separate rooms. No wonder.*

'Do you know where he might b-b-be?'

'He must've stayed with a patient at the Elephant and Castle. Sheffield, you know?' she half questioned, half-insinuated, with a flourish of her right arm. Before Billings could answer, she slammed the door.

'Thanks, you old bat,' he said to himself.

Billings returned to his horse and led it across the street to the hotel. Finding the doctor and bartender slumped in chairs at one of the tables, sound asleep, he coughed. This startled the barman, and he wobbled to his feet, very unsteadily. He reached over the table to his drinking companion and shook West's arm. The old man stirred a little but did not lift his head off the table.

'What do you want?' the barman asked in a slurred voice.

'I need the doctor. Captain Allen has been injured bad, and W-W-W-West has to come with me to Blayney,' Billings answered.

The barman again shook West's arm, and with a start, as if torn from a wonderful dream, West lifted his head.

'D-D-Doctor West, you have to come with me,' Billings blurted.

'Like hell I do!' exclaimed West and deposited his head back on the table.

'S-S-S-Sir, I – I mean, that is, the C-C-Captain is wounded, and we have to go to B-B-B-Blayney.' The boy's stutter obviously became much worse when he was under pressure. He moved to West and also shook him.

'Get off, I'll kill you if you...' West gained his feet and immediately fell at Billings's.

Billings was taken by surprise but quickly grabbed West's slumped body under the arms and tried to lift him. The best he could do was position West against the leg of the table.

'We must get him into a cart. I'll go to the camp and get one. Y-Y-You get some coffee into him, and I'll be back,' Billings ordered. He wasn't usually so forceful or decisive, but his leader was badly injured, and he was going to do everything in his power to get help.

Leaving the bar, he mounted and rode to the barracks as quickly as his exhausted mount could carry him.

Around half an hour later, Billings arrived back at the Elephant with two other soldiers. They entered and found West sitting in a chair being plied with hot coffee by the mistress of the house.

'Come. Now,' Billings ordered. When West ignored him, he gestured to his two helpers, who bodily lifted the man, carried him out the door and almost threw him onto a buckboard they had prepared.

West sat up in the pouring rain and projectile vomited over the nearest soldier.

'Oh, Christ!' the man exclaimed. He quickly moved to the horse trough and submerged his arm to wash off the offensive liquid.

West fell backwards into the blanket pile which had been placed for Allen to be brought back in comfort. A light pigskin waterproof cover lay over it, and another was thrown over West.

Billings climbed the front of the wagon and took the reins. Another of the men settled next to him. The third, smelling strongly of alcohol, mounted his own horse, and the group headed for Blayney.

Chapter 19

FOR THE RETURN journey to Bathurst, Allen was positioned on the back of the buckboard in as comfortable a position as possible. He travelled with West, one of the other wounded soldiers, and Poole's body, which had been tightly bound in hides procured from the widow at Blayney.

He knew there was a fair chance that the wound on his back would become infected and allowed all the 'fussing' that the soldiers, led by Gayner, lavished upon him. Never having been a drinking man, he took brandy from West and swigged it down as quickly as he was able.

The rain still fell, and the entire district was being drenched. The ground was sodden, and travel was extremely slow. The horses walked with their heads down, as if it were going to help keep the water out of their eyes.

There was still only one passable crossing of the Macquarie River. The party had skirted several other entry points to the town, knowing they would be unpassable. They were able to move through a low but very wide part of the flood plain and, late in the afternoon, arrived at the now flooded ford. The waters had swallowed the road for hundreds of yards, and it was now far too dangerous to use.

Aware there would be difficulty in getting to the settlement at Napoleon Reef, and also aware the waters were still rising, Gayner decided that the group would have to go to one of the local farms to wait. Sheffield's farm was the first port of call, but they could get nowhere near the main part of the property. The river, where it had been dammed, had flooded. The buildings were, they later learned, completely inundated.

'We'll have to go up to Brucedale,' Gayner said. 'If we can get that far.'

He moved to Allen and apprised him of the situation. Allen simply nodded. He was chilled to the bone, and it was obvious he had to hand control to Gayner. This didn't worry him; he'd been in many scrapes with Gayner and the rest of the troop and had no doubt they were doing everything within their power to keep him safe.

It was almost midnight when the bedraggled group reached the Douglas property. They found it impossible to get to the house, as the river had taken the front fence and, with the two front dams, had become part of the raging torrent.

Gayner, knowing that Allen's life was at stake, ordered three of the troop to dismount and cut a hole through Brucedale's front fence. This allowed them to go around the water and come up the hill to the house. Gayner himself rode ahead to beg assistance and harbour from the Douglases.

George answered the knock with his rifle raised but put the weapon back behind the door when he recognised the visitor. Gayner quickly informed him of the plight of Allen and the other wounded men. George instructed that the wounded be brought to the house while the rest of the troop set up camp in the hay shed just behind the main barn. This carried out, Sarah set about cooking for the whole crew, and soon, the aroma of freshly baked food could be smelt by all.

Allen was laid on the couch in the front room, and the flickering flames were built up to a roaring, bright fire. He was shivering. Martin and George found several blankets and, taking the man's drenched clothing, wrapped him tightly to raise his temperature.

West was treating the two other men on the front veranda; Sarah opened the door and asked him to bring them in. She'd made room in the front bedroom and instructed Carter to build up its fire. West nodded. He too was shivering, as the rain had seeped through his old leather coat, and it was wetter on the inside than out.

Carter moved the group to the floor in the main bedroom, with everyone present helping. He and Leo soon had the open fire roaring.

The three boys were then sent out to see if the rest of the troop were settled and return with wood for the fires.

As the three entered the hay shed, they could see only one of the soldiers. The others had climbed in among the hay, covered themselves with their coats and blankets, and drawn hay over the top. The man standing was Billings. He shook hands with the three boys in turn and thanked them for their assistance.

There being no way of heating the shed, James and Leo went to the main barn and found as many hessian sacks as they could. They returned and handed them to Billings. He moved to each of the soldiers and distributed the extra layers of cloth. All were thankful. The boys returned to the house with as much timber as they could carry and laid it next to the hearth in the lounge, then returned to the shed for another load.

Sarah and Willow had soon made a round of scones and sent a dozen out to the shed with the boys, Sarah saying, 'Tell the men I'll have some meat cooked as soon as I can – oh, and bread, and some eggs.' She was mentally working out what she had to offer.

Allen sat up on the couch, George and Martin warming him with their body heat. Between them, they fed Allen and gave him hot tea. He was thankful but exhausted. Sarah also made food available to the men in the house, and West sat at the table sampling everything that came out of the oven. He turned down the tea, supplementing the repast with brandy from his own flask.

By about three in the morning, everyone had eaten their fill, and the kitchen went into shutdown. The two women had toiled for several hours and knew that all had appreciated their efforts.

The morning light came late, it seemed, as the dark, heavy clouds were still dumping their load on the area. Willow emerged first and moved to the henhouse in the backyard to collect as many eggs as she could. The twenty laying hens had done their best, but she knew there wouldn't be enough for everyone.

Re-entering the kitchen, she found Sarah washing plates from the previous night's meal. Within a few minutes, the two had new bread on the go and bacon sizzling on every part of the stovetop. There were more than a dozen to feed, and they meant to do the best they could for the visitors first, then the family would eat.

Sam soon came into the room, always being the earliest riser of the men, and as if it were natural, began to wipe the plates. Within the next half an hour, the other two boys and Carter were also helping, buttering fresh bread and preparing meat from the cold room for cooking. Among the many trades Carter had turned his hand to was butchery, and he sliced and diced mutton and the best part of a hindquarter of beef not only for breakfast but for the next few days. He had, like the rest of the family, realised the visitors weren't going to be able to leave for several days after the rain ceased.

The downpour didn't clear completely for two more days, and it was another seven before the party could go to Bathurst. By the sixth day, Allen was well enough to tell the story of the tracking and ambush of the Wiradjuri. He said he was very proud of his men and how they had conducted themselves.

The family glared as if transfixed, having no wish to hear the story. However, when he mentioned that the leader had disappeared, they all thought of Jaiemba and hoped he'd been saved by the missing tracker.

The three boys got up as one and left the room, followed by Carter and the two women. They were all disgusted. Those were friendly people, and now they had been destroyed like wild animals.

The boys discussed the matter with Carter. He was unable to assuage their hatred toward Allen and his men, and they decided to treat these 'visitors' as coldly as they could. Though there was no similar organised protest by the adults, there were few pleasantries, other than food, offered to the soldiers while they remained at Brucedale.

The boys prepared the horses and cart for the trip to Bathurst as quickly and curtly as they could and then made themselves scarce when thanks and goodbyes were offered by Allen. The adults stood in front of the house, nodding as the mounted party passed. They knew the soldiers had only done what they were ordered to do, but each had great empathy for the fallen, and there was no exaltation offered.

Transport from the east side of the river was now being conducted by boat, and the men were moved a few at a time, the wounded first with West, to the Bathurst side. The horses had to be left behind in a paddock near the crossing point. One soldier, Billings, remained to look after them.

The men who conducted the crossings were doing a roaring trade, taking as much money as they could for the pleasure. Even floods were good for those with no conscience.

Chapter 20

THE TERRIBLE FATE of the Wiradjuri at the hands of the murderous group headed by Sheffield Junior, and later by the soldiers, had affected the family at Brucedale. The boys, in particular, found it hard to bury their loathing of the deeds committed and the lack of justice shown to the Wiradjuri.

George spoke to them the day after the soldiers left and tried to calm their bitterness. This was extremely hard, as he felt the same bitterness, and could see in his mind's eye the dead child still clinging to its mother's breast.

'I think we all knew Jaiemba and his men would be killed,' he started, and the words quavered in his throat. He paused to regain his composure. 'It is unfair, I know... but, um, the soldiers are not to blame.'

'I don't believe Jaiemba is dead,' James said, and a tear that he'd been fighting tracked down his cheek.

'I hope you're right, son. There's no way for us to tell. When good people do terrible things, even if they have good reason...'

George could not finish the sentence. A few moments passed, and he chose his words a little more carefully, saying, 'The followers of Sheffield Junior killed by Jaiemba and his men perhaps deserved their fate, but the others whose lives were taken, and those who lost their husbands and fathers, did not. Their lives are forever changed, their hatred of the Wiradjuri forever imprinted on their minds.'

He took time to settle and added, 'We know what started this terrible mess... but many will only see what happened through blinkered eyes.'

'Well, we must make the truth known, no matter what,' Sam answered, and his father was so proud of him that he hugged the boy tightly. George signalled to the other two boys. All four embraced, and tears were shed, but none of them felt ashamed.

Over the next few days, George attempted to be heard locally on several occasions but was always stymied by members of the grieving families or Harley and his ilk. He thought he'd have better luck with Parliament itself. He'd written to the governor and had received no response. Previously, he'd made the acquaintance of John Burton, who stood in the seat where his original farm had been, Baulkham Hills. Burton had bought the farm when George had decided to sell and given quite a good sum of money.

George wrote to Burton, who invited him to attend a sitting of the House. Not sure how attending would help, George had first thought to refuse, but at Sarah's insistence, he decided that it would, at least, be a good time for his boys to see the larger world.

After a few days, he accepted the invitation, and they arrived at Parliament House in Sydney two days prior to the sitting, just two weeks later. The grand building was an amazing sight for the three boys who'd accompanied him. Coming to its front, they were met by an attendant and conducted to the small office of John Burton, who was waiting for them.

'Well, George,' he said, as he rose from his chair and took George by the hand, 'who are these fine young men?'

'My two sons James and Samuel, and my adopted son Leo,' George answered.

The boys in turn stepped up to shake Burton's hand. Leo glowed; he had never been so introduced. As if rehearsed, each retired to stand behind their father.

'You've been causing quite a stir out in the sticks,' Burton stated.

He paused, waiting for a reply which was not forthcoming. There was a short and awkward silence, then he added, 'Your local mayor, Harley, er... something, has written me a long letter stating that you are a rabblerouser and should be ignored.'

Still receiving no response, he continued, 'I tend to think everything that man says is meant to make him money. Can't stand him. You, however, I have the greatest confidence in. A self-made man, and, I must say, you sold me a wonderful farm for a very reasonable price.'

George thought it time to break his silence and said, 'You offered a more than fair price, and others tried to take it for a steal.'

'Yes, I try to pay for what I get. It's good for everyone to see how business should be conducted.'

Being a true politician, he liked the sound of his own voice. Though George hadn't really thought of him as a friend, he did trust the man.

'We sit the day after tomorrow from ten am. I'll announce the subject for which you are to be heard,' he said, with some pageantry, and looked into George's eyes. George gasped.

'What? You expect me to stand in front of the parliament and speak?'

'Yes, that's the only place you can and should be heard.' Burton had a wry smile on his face.

'Oh, no, that's not what I intended. I am not a learned man. They would laugh me out the front door,' George answered, most surprised by this turn of events.

'I have provided a time for you to be heard, and heard you will be,' Burton instructed. Then, seeing how uncomfortable George looked, he added, 'You'll be fine. You're quite a good speaker, from what I've been told.'

The three boys looked at each other, beaming with pride. Sam, seeing that George was wavering, stepped forward and said, 'This is a great opportunity, Father. You must do it.'

'But I'm dressed like a farmer. I could never go in there looking like this.' He gestured to his clothes.

'A good man would understand that the clothing on your back does not make you, but if it bothers you so much, I could lend you a suit,' Burton offered.

'Oh, but why would they listen to me?' George questioned.

'There are a great deal of good men in the House, and they will hear you. They may not have the numbers to vote any action through, but they will hear you, and make others listen as well.' Burton paused. 'They need to hear it from you.'

'Yes, they do!' exclaimed Sam.

'This young man would do it for you if he could.' Burton laughed.

'Sorry, sir, I didn't mean to speak out of turn,' Sam said.

'I hear in your voice the possibility, the *possibility*, that you will become a leader among men. I can see why your father appears proud when he hears you speak.' Burton nodded to George. 'You have a fine young man here, George, and you should listen to him.'

George had lowered his head, unsure of himself, but he lifted his eyes to his sons and realised that they all expected him to do this dreaded thing. 'Yes, he would speak, and probably do a better job than me,' he answered and then raised his head, as he could see how proud the boys were of him. 'I will speak.'

'Good, good,' Burton said. 'That is decided, then. I have a few people in my pocket who will see that you are heard. Would you like help with the speech?'

'Well, I think I'd be better speaking off the cuff, not reading some prepared thing,' George said and looked long into Burton's face. 'What do you think?'

'Yes, I think it's always more impressive if one can orate without text. Perhaps a few notes? I always write the names on my hand when I intend to refer to people. I would also come dressed as you are; don't try to be someone who puts on airs. The offer of a suit still stands, though, if it will make you feel more at ease.'

Burton's meandering way of speaking in statements and then in questions left George a bit bewildered. He paused for a moment and said, 'I think I will come as myself.'

'Good, good. Meet me here in the morning, and we'll get ready to go in. What about the lads?'

'Oh, I hadn't thought of that. Where can they go in the building?' George asked.

'Well, actually, they aren't allowed in the public gallery unless they're accompanied by an adult, but we're in luck. My secretary just happens to be an adult. I'll see if he's able to look after the boys and get them into the House for your speech. How does that sound?'

'That would be fine, if the boys are happy?' George looked questioningly at the three bright young faces, all nodding agreement.

Burton said, in a politician's voice, 'If you elicit the right response, I will be the first man to stand and move some sort of action. If they do not listen to reason, I'll try to act on this in the future. You're a good citizen, George. Don't be overawed by the surroundings; you deserve to be heard. Remember that. You deserve to be heard.'

The men shook hands, and Burton led the family into an adjoining office, which was the size of a box room, to meet his secretary.

'This is Mr George Douglas; he'll be speaking in the House when we sit, as you know, and his boys need to be in the gallery to watch. Can you accompany them and bring them back here to await our return?' Burton asked in his rambling way, then when his subordinate had nodded and written his instructions down, Burton turned and introduced him as Hayward Williams.

George stepped forward and took Williams by the hand. 'Thank you. I appreciate your assistance.'

'It will be my pleasure,' he answered in what could only have been a Welsh accent; it was the broadest George had heard since he was a young man at the orphanage. The gardener there spoke with the sing-song patter for which the Welsh were so well known.

The boys looked at each other, then Sam said, 'Thank you, sir. We will give you no trouble, and we appreciate your time.'

Williams's smile was almost as broad as his accent, and he added, with a little nod of his head to Sam, 'At your service.'

They departed the House, the biggest building they'd ever been in, still in awe of its grandeur and the importance of its combatants.

Two days later, the boys rose in the room next to their father's in the People's Palace. They had a more than adequate pair of rooms, which shared a bathroom with six others.

James knocked on his father's door and entered on an instruction from within. George looked somewhat dishevelled; his hair was undone, and he wore only pants and a shirt, which he hadn't yet buttoned. The shirt was white, and the boys only saw him wear these clothes, his Sunday best, to funerals and weddings.

Sam noticed some notes on the table and asked, 'Have you written a speech, then?'

George answered, 'No. I tried to, but nothing would come. I made a few notes, though.'

'What a great day it will be. I wish Mother was here to see you in parliament.'

'Perhaps, if they even listen to me.'

'You always know what to say,' Sam reassured him. 'We're always proud of you. They will listen.'

George was imbued with gratitude. Sam meant what he said, and though George had little confidence in his own ability to do the task, he didn't doubt the support of his boys for a moment.

Sam helped him dress and tie his thin black tie, which looked best fit for a funeral. His shoes, though, were as immaculate as they could be. One thing he had always impressed upon the boys was that they might not have the best of everything, but they could at least look after what they did have.

On reaching the front steps of Parliament House, they met and shook hands with Burton and Williams.

'Good luck,' each of the boys said, and they parted.

George went inside, feeling a little like a lamb to the slaughter. Williams led the boys to a small shop at the corner of Pitt Street. There, he ordered a coffee and asked the boys what they would have to drink. Sam answered first, saying water would be fine, and the other two nodded. Williams laughed and ordered three large glasses of milk. He sat drinking with the wide-eyed trio as they took in the city bustling around them.

They wasted an hour at the shop, and when Williams had finished his second cup, he led them back to Parliament House. They entered, this time, through the rear, as there was a build-up of important people on the front steps. Among them was Charles Cowper, the Premier of New South Wales, who had earlier brought in the Land Acts of 1861, which sought to open Crown land and break the squatters' monopoly. Cowper was loved by some but hated by many for this act. Now, he looked a rather frail individual, but when he passed the boys, they were surprised at his stature. He seemed to be head and shoulders above the other men who clustered around him. He had one of the most impressive beards they had ever seen.

Once inside, the group moved to Williams's office and sat quietly awaiting the great moment. Around an hour later, the call came that the House had been seated, and Williams led the boys to the public gallery, where they could see the great and not-so-great of New South Wales.

Burton was positioned two seats from his leader, and Cowper beamed around the room, obviously in command. There were no parties in parliament at this time, but men of like mind to Cowper sat to the right of the Speaker, and the followers of Henry Parkes sat to the left. Some minor trivial business was conducted, and after about forty minutes, the moment the boys had waited for came, as George was introduced by Burton.

'If it pleases the House, I invite to the floor George Douglas,' he said. 'Mr Douglas comes to us all the way from Bathurst with news of a terrible injustice. I have known the honourable gentleman for around ten years, and I believe he has news we all need to hear.'

The House was attentive as George, who hadn't previously been visible to the boys, came to the lectern.

'I give you George Douglas,' Burton concluded. A call of 'Hear, hear!' echoed from his side of the room as he re-seated himself, nodding to George.

George, looking like a fish out of water, placed his small bundle of papers on the lectern and looked up and around the room. In a broken and quiet voice, he began, 'Thank you to the member Mr Burton, and to all of you for listening to what I have to say.'

One of the members said loudly, 'Speak up, man.'

George straightened his shirt and stood a little taller as he added, in a much bolder voice,

'I am here to report on awful events which have recently taken place in the Bathurst area. The local Wiradjuri are being driven to extinction.'

He faltered again and then continued, with some interjections challenging his expertise to make such assertions.

'I recently witnessed one such event. Pictures I still see in my mind's eye move me. A waterhole poisoned and more than a dozen women, old men and children all lying dead.'

He paused and found that now, the members were all silent.

'My strongest and most haunting memory is that of a young mother lying dead in the dried mud with her small child still at her breast.' George wiped a tear. Several of the members thought it was well rehearsed, but still none spoke.

Fumbling with his papers, George regained his equilibrium and continued. 'These people were here before us. They have lived off this hard land for perhaps thousands of years.'

This statement drew some comments from the floor, and the words 'terra nullius' were murmured.

'Yes, I have heard the term,' George said loudly, and the mumbling died down again. 'Even if we think they were not farming the land, we cannot say they were not here. It seems we have the power to destroy these people and that is what we are about to do.'

The House descended into chaos, shouts echoing from both sides.

'The elderly, women and children were tricked into using a poisoned waterhole, which is now unusable, perhaps for generations. The Wiradjuri men were off looking for water and food. When they returned to find the terrible scene, they were driven, as I think we all would be, to seek revenge.'

This created an uproar, and Burton stood and addressed the Speaker.

'Sir, I recommend that you direct the House be silent. They may learn something.'

The deliberate provocation was intended to take some of the heat off George.

'I will thank you to remember who is in the chair and keep your recommendations to yourself,' the Speaker stated, slamming his gavel once.

'I was not intending to pressure the Honourable Speaker, but these truths need to be heard.'

The Speaker tapped his gavel once more and said, 'Resume your seat, and the House will be silent while our guest delivers his speech. You will all have time to speak at its conclusion.'

The murmuring lessened somewhat, and George, now finding his ire rising, spoke with a louder orator's voice. 'The men of the tribe killed several people who they blamed for the murder of their families.'

This caused raised voices from both sides. One said, 'This is nothing to do with murder; they deserved what they got.' Another voice blurted, 'For shame, for shame!' and yet another uttered loudly, echoing the earlier statement, 'They're little more than animals, killing good white men...'

This enraged George, who regarded his upbringing as akin to the way the Wiradjuri were treated. He knew oppression of the masses back in England and the entitlement of the rich and royal.

'"Good white people" is not how I would describe those murderers. These were human beings they massacred, not wild animals. They had no right to just kill them.'

The uproar continued, and the Speaker stood banging his gavel to little avail.

'If they poisoned your wife and children, would you not take up arms?' yelled George, losing patience with the recalcitrant members.

He thought, *I am not lesser than some in this chamber*. Now he had his flow going, and he was not about to be shouted down by a few whose sense of entitlement drove their need to be seen as protectors of the 'poor, set-upon white people' of Bathurst and, indeed, the greater state.

'Good men cannot stand by while these terrible events are happening,' George stated, and the general sounds of disapproval quieted somewhat. 'The warriors of the tribe were ambushed and killed, and two other unrelated groups have been slaughtered since.'

George calmed himself and, after a moment, added, 'Soon, there will be no Wiradjuri people in the area, and we will have, in the period of a generation, wiped them out. For shame.'

The House was quiet and came to complete silence as Henry Parkes stood, waiting to be heard. Silence achieved, the Speaker too arose and said, 'The right honourable Sir Henry Parkes.'

'I have some sympathy with your cause, Mr Douglas, but what do you wish us to do... after the events?'

'I think we should start a dialogue with the Wiradjuri and other tribes,' George answered.

This again caused an outcry; one voice was heard to say 'Preposterous!' Though there were many other comments, none were audible, with so many all shouting at once.

'They are people and deserve to be treated the same under the law as any man,' George said loudly, and consequently, the shouting grew even more furious.

Parkes stood once more and waited for the quiet his status demanded. When the room became silent, he began, 'But the law does not recognise the Aborigines as equal beings.' Several members shouted support for his comment, and he raised a hand to calm their pernicious comments. 'We have fought to stop the transportation of convicts from England. We have fought to become our own masters. So, why is it so hard to fight for these people, before they are all gone?'

Burton stood and, on being recognised, said, 'We hold these truths to be self-evident, that all men are created equal,' a reference to the American Declaration of Independence.

The quote went too far for many, and comments of 'We are not bloody Americans!' and, perhaps less articulately, 'Traitor!' met with calls of 'For shame!' from those opposite.

Parkes motioned for silence, and the room became hushed for a few moments. Then there was an outbreak of vile language as the indignant on Parkes's own side protested uproariously.

They were met by yelling from the other side of the table, with comments being mostly inaudible; some, however, took to shouting 'For shame!' again, and other such provocative taunts.

Cowper now rose and reached across the table to Parkes, who took the handshake in the symbolic manner in which it was offered. Some gasps were heard, and then some clapping and a few cheers, but the loudest noises were still those in opposition to anything which could be seen as supporting the Aboriginal cause.

Many still believed that the white man had some 'God-given' right to rule. Some would never give either Parkes or Cowper a future vote in the House. It was seen by many to be selling out their birthright and the supremacy believed to be an Englishman's entitlement.

George stood for a short time listening to the inane babbling coming from those he'd imagined to be respected leaders of the land. He was disgusted and thought how small and loathsome some of them seemed. He was about to step away from the lectern when Burton, obviously not wishing to miss an opportunity to speak, stood and waved a hand at the Speaker.

'I will not be waved at like a hansom cab driver,' the Speaker said indignantly.

'I'm sorry, Mr Speaker. I only meant to attract your attention through all of the rabble,' Burton answered.

This raised the stakes even more, and shouting again drowned out the sensible comments from the room. The Speaker stood and banged his gavel as hard as he could until the room grew at least somewhat quieter.

'The Honourable Sir John Burton has the call,' he ordered.

'Thank you, Mr Speaker,' Burton said. 'I believe Mr Douglas deserves better than he has received here today.'

More shouts came, but it was somewhat quieter.

'He travelled all the way across the Blue Mountains to speak here, and he has not been given due deference.'

Again, a few comments were shouted, though it seemed the members were beginning to agree, overall, that Burton was correct. He continued, 'I, for one, should like to hear what our honourable visitor has to say.'

He looked at the public gallery and received some applause. He noted that the three boys and Williams led the clapping.

'There seems to be hatred in some minds for the Aboriginal people and for the Wiradjuri in particular.' A few murmurs continued. 'I recommend Mr Douglas to the House,' Burton concluded and sat down. Several of the members, including Cowper and Parkes, clapped their approval.

George looked to his boys and could see that they were willing him on. He straightened his shirt again and said, 'These people are being persecuted, poisoned at waterholes, shot like stray dogs, and hanged by the side of the road, often for something they had nothing to do with in the first place.'

He paused. Silence had gripped the room. He nodded as if answering his own statement and continued, 'Yes, they are being eradicated like feral animals. I've had a lot to do with these people. I look to my sons in the gallery and see one there who was saved by the Wiradjuri when he was lying, badly injured, in a paddock far from the homestead. They treated him, fed him, and brought him home. A child is alive because of their care and kindness. And how are they repaid for that kindness? Their elders, women and children poisoned and left to die, their men hunted down and slaughtered. I see in my mind's eye that scene at the waterhole. I cannot rest until they receive justice. I see the child still at its mother's breast... dead... and I hear jeering in this place. For shame, for shame.'

His voice broke and quavered as emotion gripped him. The room remained hushed.

'Imagine yourself in the place of these people. Would you herald the day the white man came to your land, or would you hate it? I have seen Wiradjuri trackers used to hunt men of their own race. Without trial, without even giving them the chance to speak for themselves. I have seen many put to work as slaves in New South Wales, many years after slavery was abolished in the British Empire.'

He took a long pause, hearing his own voice echo back to him from the walls of the huge room. 'Our queen, God bless her, has spoken against slavery, and most right-thinking countries have abolished the practice. These are not animals; these are men and women with a long and proud history in this land. I ask this place to see the wrongs being done, being done in the name of a false belief that white people have an innate right to take anything they like and persecute anyone who cannot defend him or herself. I call on you, our leaders, to lead, and to challenge these terrible acts at every turn. I call on you all here today to outlaw the killing and serve justice to these members of Queen Victoria's empire.'

There was a short pause as many thought what to do, then Parkes and Cowper stood as one and clapped loudly. Their allies followed, and soon, most of the members were standing and applauding George Douglas. The boys in the gallery were also standing, tears of joy, tears of pride, running down their cheeks.

Burton stood, rushed to George and took him by the hand. Cowper and Parkes followed the action in turn, as did their immediate supplicants. After a short time, the Speaker descended from his chair, also shaking George's hand.

Almost twenty minutes later, the House was called to order. Though no immediate action was taken on George's speech, time would see the practice of slavery and the unlawful, indiscriminate killing of Aboriginal people gradually outlawed.

George was eventually elected mayor of the Bathurst jurisdiction. He served three consecutive terms. He resisted courting by both Parkes and Robertson and, some years later, by Edmund Barton, the country's first prime minister.

Barton travelled in 1902 to Brucedale to see if he could convince George that he was needed in the next government. George and his family greeted him with great warmth, and Sam spoke to him with an eloquence far above his age and experience. Barton was disappointed by George's refusal but revelled in the beauty of a good rainy season, which saw the paddocks as green as they ever became in the area. He joked that he should, perhaps, be there to enlist Sam for the next term.

All laughed at the thought, but secretly, Sam was longing to take his place in either the state or Commonwealth government. Like his father, he impressed Barton, who remembered him a few years on, when Andrew Fisher prepared to form government a second time, and recommended Sam for a position.

Sam jumped at the chance and was duly elected in 1910. Soon after, he was given a Cabinet position with an eye to the Treasury. He excelled in the role and made many speeches in Melbourne, where parliament sat at the time.

Sam only served two three-year terms, as his second term saw the Fisher Government voted down and in opposition. Sam felt that he was wasting his time and returned home to Bathurst.

In 1905, Sheffield passed away at his own hand. He had never really recovered from his son's death and wasted away until he decided to use his revolver to end his own suffering. No relatives survived him, and to the surprise of all in the area, he left his farm, all of his belongings and a large sum of money to George Douglas.

George was called, along with several witnesses, to the reading of the will, and was left speechless when his name was read as beneficiary. He could say nothing at all when Solicitor White asked how he would like the money invested.

After examining the will himself, he could see that everything was in order. He had spoken to Sheffield the week before his death and observed nothing in his countenance to suggest that he was about to end his life. Though they saw each other most weeks, there was little conversation between them about money matters, and he had certainly never let on that he was leaving anything to George.

On returning to Brucedale, the now eighty-year-old George spent time in his bedroom with Sarah discussing what to do next. They both felt that the Sheffield spread was grander than they needed, and though they knew the money would make life much easier, neither of them wanted to leave the home they had built this late in life.

At the evening meal, George stood and formally announced to the family what Sheffield had done. Everyone sat with mouths agape, and nothing was said for several minutes.

George was still standing as he said, 'We have decided that James will run this farm from next year.' He paused to examine the look in each of the boys' eyes. He saw no surprise and no dissent. The three knew this was the right thing to do, as James was, for all intents and purposes, running things already.

George nodded as they all watched on quietly. 'Sarah and I want you, Martin and Willow, to take the Sheffield property.' Quickly, he raised a hand to stop Martin from replying. 'We have lived with you and used you as workers without ever giving you a real wage. This is fair, and I know everyone here will think so.'

'If I may, Father?' Sam said, receiving George's nod of approval. 'This is the right thing to do. I've made a considerable amount of money and would never have wanted any land. I'm more interested in living in the city and may go back into politics at a state level in the future. James deserves this property. He will, most likely, make it the best in the district.'

He paused, then continued. 'Martin, you and Willow are more than our greatest friends; you truly are our family, and you'll make wonderful neighbours. I'll have a second home to visit when I return to Bathurst. I think it's the most perfect thing that could happen.'

Beaming, he reached for Martin's hand, and shook it, but Martin was ready to refuse the offer when James also took his hand.

'I'm delighted. You deserve this, and I know you'll make a go of it,' James said.

George took back the floor. 'I wasn't finished,' he stated. 'Part of the inheritance includes the old Wilson property, and that we are giving to you, Leo.'

Leo looked startled and shook his head uncertainly, but George reassured him that the eighty acres would need Carter to help stock and run the place. He knew Carter was now past his best, but Leo would look after him in his dotage.

James swung around to Leo, who he truly did think of as a brother, and gave him a hug. Sam moved to the two and embraced them together.

'We're giving you a thousand pounds to start your herd with, and we're giving you, Carter, another thousand in back wages,' George said.

Everyone in the room beamed. Martin said, 'I thank you for your generosity, but I'm happy just helping you.'

Willow took his hand. 'We love you all as our family, the only family we've ever had, really.' A tear rolled down her cheek. 'We don't need a farm. We have you all.'

Sarah embraced her. 'You need to take this. We don't need it, and we want you to have your own home.'

Both women wept. George again took Martin's hand and instructed, 'Accept.'

Martin was momentarily speechless, then said, 'If we do, then we'll leave it to you three boys in our will.'

George nodded, and everyone took turns embracing each other.

This was truly one of the happiest times the family ever knew. George had given more than half of the Sheffield fortune away, and he was delighted. He had more than enough money and needed nothing but to spend a quiet, satisfied old age at Brucedale.

The family prospered throughout the next two years, until 1907, when George and Sarah passed away within weeks of each other. Sarah nursed George till his death from pneumonia caused by influenza, then succumbed to the same fate. It was as if Sarah lost her will to live when she lost her wonderful partner. They'd both had good lives and could have wanted for nothing in their old age. Their boys were all successful and happy, with wives and children of their own.

In 1909, Martin passed away after a fall from his horse. To the last, he worked to make the property George had bestowed upon him the best in the area. He knew he was doing this for the boys whom he loved dearly.

Willow moved from the big house at the old Sheffield property to Brucedale. James's wife of fifteen years had just had twins, obviously a family trait. Willow was a wonderful help until her passing in 1911.

She left her property to the three boys, as instructed by Martin. She, too, had buried all the demons of her youth.

Chapter 21

LATE IN 1928, James called on the new doctor and was shocked when his wife said, 'There was a darkie looking for you at the store this morning. All dressed in a flash suit, like real people. What a hide.'

'Looking for me?' James asked, and though the woman kept talking, she did not immediately answer his question.

'And with an upper-class English accent, if you don't mind.'

'You said he was looking for me?' James put in.

'Didn't even give his name, just came up and stood next to me at the counter. The cheek!'

James, getting quite annoyed with the old biddy, asked, 'What did he want?'

'Well, I don't go sticking my nose into other people's business, but he was looking for you and you alone,' she answered, looking put out, as she regularly did.

'Did you give him my information?' James asked.

'I didn't speak to him at all... Like real people, he was.'

James, irritated by her racist attitude, left the surgery and headed for the general store. The storeman met him at the door and immediately started to tell him about the 'gentleman' who'd been seeking him earlier in the day.

'He was a fine-looking man, quite old, with grey hair. I thought he may be from India or Ceylon. Well, he asked for your family, George in fact, and I let him know your father had passed away. He seemed very disappointed until I informed him that you were still at Brucedale.' He waited for James to react.

'Where is he now?' James dutifully asked.

'Well, I set him up at the Elephant, a room for two nights. I told him I'd get in contact with you as soon as I could, and he said he would wait at the hotel.'

'Thanks,' James said and left the store, headed for the Elephant and Castle. He was directed to Room Six and wasted no time heading up the stairs and knocking. An elderly gentleman fitting the description he had been given answered the door.

'Hello, sir. My name is James Douglas, and I believe you have been asking about my family?'

'Yes, sir. My name is Rajiv Arya. Please come in.' He bowed slightly and backed away from the door, allowing his guest to enter. 'Please be seated,' he said, and James obeyed, sitting on a chair in front of a small table. Large sheets of paper were spread out on its surface. James could see a map of Australia, one of New South Wales, and other legal-looking documents which had little meaning to him.

'Sir, I've heard that you have lost your father. I was here to visit him, which is why I've asked you to come here,' Rajiv started.

James was amazed by his wonderful and cultured voice. 'Did you know my father?'

'No, no, I did not have that privilege, but I am here representing your cousin Agnes Douglas.'

'I'm sorry. I didn't even know I had a cousin,' James said in a surprised voice.

'She was the most wonderful person I've ever been able to call my friend.' He looked James up and down. 'I can see the family likeness. Agnes was the daughter of your father's brother, Henry.'

'Oh, yes. My father used to tell us of his two brothers, Henry and William. I've named my two sons after them.' A grin lit James's face as he thought of his father.

'Well, your uncle Henry became a doctor and came to India with the British East India Company. My mother was the family ayah. That is, she looked after the children, you understand?'

James nodded, and Rajiv continued. 'I was best friends with your cousin Edward. We did everything together until the terrible events of 1856.' He lowered his head as if giving deference to long-departed friends.

James tilted his head and then, seeing the emotion in Rajiv's face, remained silent and allowed him to take his time. Rajiv, noticing, realised James knew nothing about the 'terrible events of 1856' and began to explain. 'The British East India Company used to rule India; they had their own army of several thousand British soldiers and over a million sepoy soldiers.'

James again looked for clarification.

'The sepoys were Indian men who joined and fought with the British. In 1856, they were instructed to use shells which had been prepared using pig and cow fat. This they could not do, as it offended their religious beliefs. The first British officer who was disobeyed shot one of the sepoys, and the sepoys then went on, er, what we now call a strike.'

James suddenly recalled having read about the event and said, 'Oh yes, I remember something about this. Wasn't there a fight?'

'I am sad to say that my father was a sepoy at Cawnpore, where we all lived, and he, like the other sepoys, refused to do the officers' bidding. The East India Company officers saw that the men weren't obeying orders anymore and tried to negotiate the situation, but soon, unscrupulous scoundrels took control of the strike, and it was affecting the whole northern part of the country. Agnes was away at boarding school in Wellington in the south of India, where there was little conflict.'

His voice faltered. Remembering this time was a terrible thing for anyone involved.

'The place we called home suddenly became a battlefield, and the sepoys, controlled by an evil man, encircled the British part of the town and fired cannons and rifles at its inhabitants. Many were killed in the initial assault, but the British soldiers, aided by some of the sepoys who'd remained loyal to the company, repelled the attacks until the Indian leader allowed clemency for the British to leave the town on boats. We were all led to the river and had begun to load the boats when someone fired a shot. Covers fell away from the guns which had been placed around the river, and they fired on us, men, women, and children alike.'

He paused for a few moments, emotion halting him. 'Countless died there, but when the shooting ended, those of us still alive were marched back to the town. The men were separated and taken to one of the barracks buildings. We, the women and children, were housed overnight in a residence where we treated the wounded and took everything we could use as weapons. The next day, we were taken to a place called the Bibighar. There, we were given few rations and allowed to go hungry for a long time. Then the soldiers – the British soldiers, that is – were all taken out of the barracks building and lined up. We could see what was happening. They were gunned down. All of them.'

The old man shed a few tears, and James just sat holding his hand, the least he felt he could do.

When he was able, Rajiv continued. 'We were kept penned up in the Bibighar for several days, and then the sepoys were ordered to form a perimeter around our building. They were ordered to fire into it but refused. My father was one of the men who refused to massacre unarmed women and children. A woman we knew as Begum, who was supposed to have fed us, abused the soldiers and called them cowards. Then she was given the job of getting rid of us. She went away and hired local butchers to come and kill everyone in the Bibighar.'

His emotion rose even further, and for a short time, he was unable to speak.

'Edward and I had found a hiding place. We could see everything. They killed everyone... all the women, our mothers and sisters. They cut them to pieces and threw the remains in an old well.'

Now he wept openly and said no more for several minutes. James moved and sat next to the distraught man, who eventually continued.

'After a long time, my father came to the house and found Edward and me. He took us to an area we could escape from.' He verbally stumbled here, and James noticed how much his Indian accent came out when he was distressed.

'We had to travel over a thousand miles to get to Wellington. Edward became very ill on the trip, and he died just a few days after he saw Agnes. We had to tell her what had happened at Cawnpore. It was so hard.'

Rajiv sipped some water from a glass sitting on the table to one side of the paperwork. His hand shook noticeably.

'A great man called Baggs and his wife took Agnes and I back to their home in England, and they acted as parents to both of us. We wanted for nothing, and when they passed, Agnes was left their fortune.'

He turned to look into James's eyes. 'That is why I have come here to find you. I have Agnes's will and need to inform you that I have completed most of the tasks she left for me. A great deal of money was left to her school and to people who helped Edward and I get to Wellington. Half of the fortune was left to your father and his brother.'

He paused a moment and then said, 'Your uncle William immigrated to Australia.'

James interrupted here. 'We never had contact with him. Father thought him long dead.'

'No, no, he lived in Queensland. He died and left a wife and three children, then his wife also died. I have not been able to find the children.'

A long moment passed so James could digest this information, then he asked, 'Where in Queensland did they live?'

Rajiv shook his head. 'I don't know. I have only the information that your uncle died in the Brisbane area.'

Again, there was a silence, until Rajiv said, 'I have a copy of Agnes's last will and testament and would like to read it to you.'

James nodded. Soon, the will was produced from the documents on the table, and Rajiv began to read.

'This is the last will and testament of Agnes Anne Douglas-Baggs.

"'I, Agnes Anne Douglas-Baggs, do hereby appoint Rajiv Arya as my true representative and executor. I leave for Rajiv the home in London and all of its contents, and a sum of ten thousand pounds. This is not negotiable. All of my other properties are to be liquidated and the monies distributed. Half shall go to my boarding school in Wellington, India, and to any of the people who helped Rajiv and my brother Edward to reach me. This will be delivered as a money order to the school, and as cash to the others mentioned by Rajiv at his discretion. All the residual money is to go to my relatives in Australia, my uncles William and George Douglas. I am not sure of their addresses, but the residual funds are to be equally divided between them, or their children if they are not living. If, after five years, these funds are not able to be distributed, any remainder is to go to Rajiv Arya with no exception.

"'I feel happy knowing that the money will assist my father's family. My family – my mother, father and three sisters – were killed while I was at the boarding school in Wellington. They were buried in a disused well, and a monument was later erected at the site. Money has already been placed in trust for a caretaker to look after the site in perpetuity.

"I have had a very full, interesting, and privileged life, and my foster family, the Baggses, made sure that I was always looked after. By far the best man I have ever known, other than my father and Doctor Baggs, is Rajiv Arya. I recommend him to anyone to whom I have left funds, as I trust him implicitly.

"I also leave my book, which explains the Cawnpore event as seen through the eyes of my then nine-year-old brother Edward, and by Rajiv, who also witnessed the massacre. Remembering such a terrible thing will make it less likely to ever happen again. Edward's small grave is near the school, and they maintain it. Every week, flowers are left for him. This is one reason I have left money to the school; also, the memories of my time there are my most prized.

"Rajiv will give the book to my nearest living relative, and they may do with it as they please. I wrote it over many years, as the demons I had from that time needed to be expelled and this was the only way I knew to let them out. I hope the events will always be remembered and the monument visited. If my family are able to do so, I wish them to travel to Cawnpore and lay a wreath from those of the Douglas family who lived, and still live.

"I sign this, my last will and testament, on the first day of August 1925.'"

Rajiv had read the will almost without taking a breath and now broke down as he heard the voice of Agnes through its pages. James hugged him and also shed a tear. He waited for Rajiv to recover, then said, 'I don't understand it, but I feel I have always known Agnes, and yet I hadn't heard her name before today. My father never had contact with either of his brothers since he was left to the care of an orphanage. I can't even remember the name of it... He so rarely spoke of those days. He and his lifelong friends were so terribly mistreated there.'

He paused, surprised by how emotional he felt. 'I'm so pleased to hear that both of my uncles had families of their own and Henry became a doctor.'

James thought of his two wonderful parents. Then, as Rajiv had not looked up, he said, 'This money isn't something we need; my brother Leo and I have done well for ourselves on our properties, and my brother Sam is a member of the New South Wales Government. I think you should take the money and give it all to William's heirs.'

Rajiv, startled, said in a disappointed voice, 'This is what Agnes wanted to happen with her inheritance, and you must not question her actions!'

'Oh, sorry, sir. I did not intend to offend you – she knew you, and obviously loved you,' James answered. 'I would not think of questioning what she has done.'

Rajiv's face became settled again as he closed his eyes, took a deep breath and said simply, 'Good, good.'

They both sat for some time, until Rajiv felt calm enough to get to the paperwork. He placed a cash order in James's hands, on which he had written the sum of two hundred and seventy thousand pounds. James gawked at Rajiv, who raised his eyebrows as if to solicit a comment.

'Oh, hell. I'll have to get the bank to divide it and give my brothers their share.'

'No, you misunderstand. This is your share. I will see that your brothers get theirs.' Rajiv smiled as James sat open-mouthed.

James thought, *This is worth much, much more than all the property Father left between us!* He raised his eyebrows, not able to speak, and Rajiv began to reassure him.

'This is one-sixth of the money left. I still hope to find your uncle's family to distribute their inheritance.'

James gasped, overwhelmed. What on earth would he do with this huge amount?

'Sir, could I get you to come to my father's home? I would like to have my family meet you.'

Rajiv nodded, and they made plans for his pickup the next day.

On his return journey, James travelled via Leo's home and invited him, his wife Robyn and their two children Mark and Mary to Brucedale the next morning, and then headed home to tell his wife Betty and their twin boys Henry and William the good news.

Very early the next day, James travelled back into Bathurst on the small four-wheeled carriage which was Betty's favourite mode of travel. When Rajiv came downstairs from his room, James was waiting in the dining room, where he insisted Rajiv have breakfast and informed him that he would need to pack and bring his bags.

'Oh, no, sir, I wish to be no trouble,' Rajiv said, but James insisted, saying that Betty had asked him to stay at the homestead for as long as he liked. Rajiv was very surprised, as even now, some years after the British Empire had abolished slavery, a 'man of colour' was seldom asked to stay in a white person's home unless he was a servant of some kind.

He returned to his room to pack and learned from the young woman at the counter that his bill had already been paid. He thought for a moment then produced a pound note and passed it over to her as a gratuity.

The girl looked at the money with astonishment; she was seldom given a tip and never such a large amount. This was almost a week's wage. Her mouth was agape as Rajiv took his suitcase, left the hotel, and found James waiting on the carriage.

James hopped down. He secured Rajiv's bag in the rear luggage shelf, then helped him board the front seat and joined him there. This again surprised Rajiv, as on trains in London, people would leave the carriage if he entered. Travelling through India, there were still segregated carriages, and the elite were never seen in the company of the unwashed masses. He smiled as he recalled him and Agnes entering a restaurant in a very wealthy part of London some years earlier, and Agnes causing quite a scene when she was told that 'servants must eat in the back room'.

On arrival at Brucedale, the carriage was greeted by Leo, the two women and several of the children. Leo's youngest, Mary, was in a cot in the house, having put up quite a protest about being awakened early. Mary was just over a year old and the apple of her parents' eyes.

The adults were all introduced, and the women were impressed with the slight bow they received from the venerable old man. On retiring to the lounge room, which James had extended the previous year, they all seated themselves in a circle on the four low couches, which were also a new purchase.

James welcomed Rajiv to the home and relinquished the floor to him in quite a formal way. Rajiv stood and moved toward the fire, where he turned and faced them.

'As I have already told Mr James, I was the lifelong friend of the wonderful Agnes Douglas, his cousin. We lived in India as children and moved to England in 1858.'

He stopped, pausing to make sure the children, who sat on the floor, understood what he was saying. 'Agnes was a most excellent friend, and we thanked the lucky stars for the Baggs family, who took us in after we left India.'

He had deliberately left out the story about Cawnpore, thinking that the children were too young to hear such terrible things. James considered this but decided to speak.

'Our children need to hear the full story. They need to know what terrible things are done in the name of racism and bigotry,' he said, and Rajiv nodded.

'I was born in Cawnpore in India; my mother was the nursemaid for the Douglases, Doctor Henry Douglas, Mrs Douglas and their children. The family had four girls and Edward, who was the youngest and my best friend. Then the trouble started.'

He faltered for a moment, shaking as his memory strained to bridge the terrible gap his psyche had built to protect him. James rose and, taking a chair from the corner, seated Rajiv so he might continue at his will.

'The East India Company ruled India in Britain's name. India was a divided land with hundreds of feudal lords, kings and princes who all wanted control. The British brought some form of stability, and it was initially embraced. By 1856, a feeling of ill will was growing as the company's soldiers were used to settle any disturbance. Local dignitaries did not want to give up power, especially in the north of the country, and some spoke of insurrection. They called themselves freedom fighters.'

Rajiv took a long breath, looking mostly at the children. 'Many thousands of India's men, including my own father, were drafted into the army under the company's direction. They were known as sepoys. They were loyal, and proud to be so, to the British, and went into battle for them whenever asked.'

He glanced at James, seated next to his wife. James nodded.

'One day in 1857, the sepoys were instructed to ready the daily cannons to be fired. When they opened the new cartridge boxes, they found that they'd been packed in animal lard. The sepoys were horrified, as they worshipped cattle, and pigs were considered unclean, so they refused to use them. One of the British officers took this as a mutiny and shot the first sepoy who had refused.'

Rajiv again took a deep breath. 'The other men present also refused, and the officer was knocked down. He felt he could not allow the loss of face and called on his senior officer to deal with the mob. This man only knew the rule of law, as he saw it, and attempted to get the rest of the garrison to fire the guns. They refused. Soon, the loss of control was evident. Almost all the sepoys stood together; they did not lower their guns when instructed, and so started a stand-off, with the British on one side and the sepoys on the other.'

Here there was a long pause as Rajiv remembered his father in his grand uniform. Looking up at the adults with tears in his eyes, he continued, 'The freedom fighters took control of the army, promising them the white men would be driven out and they would never have to do anything against their respective religions. The sepoys were used to being under someone's control and so did as the villains instructed. Later, some shooting broke out. Edward and I were in the hills, but not knowing what had happened, as quickly as our legs would carry us, we ran home.'

The rigour of the storytelling was draining Rajiv. After a few moments which he used to compose himself, he resumed his tale.

'The British general ordered all the white people and their servants to gather in the main barracks. The British soldiers, along with the few sepoys who remained loyal, set up a perimeter and protected it with their lives. There was much shooting from both sides, and countless were killed. A messenger was sent to the nearest large garrison, at Lucknow, for help. Here, Doctor Douglas and one of his daughters died, as many did, from cholera.'

'It was killing people everywhere, Father told me,' James said.

Rajiv nodded, looking very solemn. 'Having heard of the uprising, most of the sepoys throughout the north had taken up arms against the British. Lucknow was not coming to help us, and Edward and I heard the general and his staff talking about not being able to hold out much longer. We were stranded on our own, and it seemed that all was lost. We had lasted for many days. Many were killed or wounded, but the wounded still manned the barricades.

'One morning, a rich trader named Nana Sahib intervened. The British thought they would be saved, as Sahib was in their employ, receiving a regular stipend. This was not the case, as he had assumed leadership of the revolt.'

James, seeing that Rajiv was flagging, stood and exited the room, returning with a glass of water. After thanking him and taking a long drink, Rajiv continued his diatribe.

'Nana Sahib attended the barricade on his grandly attired elephant and told the general he would negotiate peace. Three men were sent to the negotiations, and after two meetings, the British were assured of safe passage to the river, where we would use boats to travel away from the conflict. An agreement was made, and we went to the river, where all was waiting for us.

'We began to board the boats. One caught fire, and one of our soldiers thought it was a trick and shot at the man he thought had lit it. There were, suddenly, many big guns shooting at us; these had been hidden on either side of the river. I think it was planned to do away with us all. One boat escaped with but a few people on board. When the firing ceased, many lay dead.'

His voice cracked. He took another sip of water and cleared his throat.

'Those of us left alive were returned to the town, where we were separated from the men. After a terrible night in a large house, we were moved to a place called the Bibighar, the place of women. In front of us, some time later, the men were stood in a line and executed.'

He was silent for around a minute and then, gathering himself, went on. 'We were kept in the building and given little food. This was a terrible time, as the women had seen their husbands and sons killed. We were starving, but Edward and I found a way to escape from the building, got food, and brought it back. My father, who'd been looking for a way to get us out of the Bibighar, helped us.

'After many days, the sepoys surrounded the building and were ordered to shoot all of us. The men refused, saying that if they would not kill sacred animals, they certainly would not kill unarmed women and children. The evil woman who'd been given the task of feeding us while we were held as hostages, who was known as Begum, ranted and raved at the sepoys, calling them cowards and many other awful names. Nana Sahib and one of his men threatened the sepoys, but having had enough, they turned their guns toward the three, ready to shoot them. My father was one of those sepoys. They were heard and marched away to one of the further barracks. We thought we were saved, but ...'

Rajiv's words trailed off. A tear fell from his well-worn cheek, and taking a deep breath, he forced himself to go on.

'Begum was ordered to kill all of us, and she left and returned with local butchers. These men were hated by most of the religious groups, as they slaughtered all animals for the food of the British and the castes who ate meat. Most were criminals who could only do this type of work. They were ordered to kill everyone; Edward and I hid but could see the women and children being killed. Everyone was killed but us.'

Now he wept openly. There were no thoughts of embarrassment, no qualms about what his audience would think. The women and children all had been showing the same emotions, and he could see how it was affecting them.

'Both of our mothers and Edward's other two sisters were among the dead.'

The women gasped, and he continued, breathing heavily, 'The next day, after some of the bodies were taken and dumped in an old well, the butchers left, having finished their evil work. After the hostages were all dead, the sepoys were released. My father took this chance to leave the barracks and to show Edward and me how to escape through the sewerage pit.

'We travelled for many weeks; Edward got more ill each day, but he was determined to get to Wellington to find his only living sister, Agnes. It was an arduous journey. We were threatened by many things and some people, but others helped us, fed us, and we made it to Wellington.'

Rajiv looked up for the first time in minutes and said, 'Agnes and I were taken to England by her father's business partner, Mr Baggs, and his wife, and raised as English children. We could never forget what had happened, though. Agnes wrote this book and sent me to find her relatives and give it to them.'

He lifted a large, tied document and handed it to James.

'She also left a large amount of money which I was asked to bring to her living relatives. You are the family of George Douglas, and I now will give you each your share of the money, as Agnes instructed.'

Rajiv moved to the table, took the cheque, which James had handed back to him the previous day, and passed it over the table to James. He handed it on to his wife. He hadn't told anyone the amount, and she gasped, the sum being more than she thought she would ever see.

Rajiv handed a second cheque to Leo. Leo immediately protested, 'But I'm not actually one of George's children.'

'Rubbish. Our father called you his son, and that's good enough for me. You are our family, as Rajiv was family to Agnes,' exclaimed James, shocked that Leo would say such a thing. Rajiv smiled through his tears.

Leo looked at the amount written on the piece of paper and fell back in his chair, turning white. 'Oh my God!' he stuttered. His wife, looking over his shoulder, gave a little whistle; she had never seen such a large figure.

Rajiv produced another cheque for two hundred and seventy thousand pounds and said, 'I have addressed this to your brother Sam. Where would I go to see that he receives it?'

'Sam lives in Sydney but will be home in Brucedale with his new wife in about a week's time. They're coming for Christmas.' James paused for a moment. 'Sir, we would be glad to have you stay with us so you can deliver the money to Sam. I hope you will accept our hospitality until then?'

'I would like to spend the time with you, but I still have William's children to find.'

'Well, if you don't mind me saying so, I think you're looking exhausted. You're more likely to get the money to the other members of our family if you take a short rest,' James said, looking for approval from his wife.

'That is settled then. You must stay,' she agreed.

Rajiv said, 'I thank you; I will think on it overnight.'

James stood and signalled to Betty. 'We'll prepare some food.'

The two left the room and moved to the kitchen. Once there, James said, 'I would like to go with Rajiv when he tries to find our cousins. What do you think?'

Betty paused for a moment, looking into his eyes, and answered,

'Of course you must go. We have enough people here to mind the farms, and Carter will care for us.'

She smiled, and he beamed back at her. He knew that Carter, now in his nineties, needed more care than he could give, but he also knew that his wife always loved looking after him. James reached for her and hugged her to him; he felt like the luckiest man in the world.

They returned to the family, who were all still in the lounge room. Rajiv now sat in one of the two rocking chairs, next to Carter, who'd gone to sleep.

James said, smiling broadly, 'Sir, if it pleases you, I would like to travel with you when you go to find my uncle William's family.'

Before Rajiv could answer, Leo said, 'I should like to go too, if that's alright?'

James nodded, delighted at his brother's commitment.

'That would take a weight off my mind,' Rajiv said. 'We may be gone for some months, though.'

Leo looked at his wife, and she showed her approval immediately.

The family, with its new member, Rajiv, waited patiently for five days until Sam, his wife Lindsay, and their newly born son Adam arrived. Lindsay was an older mother, though she was more than twenty years Sam's junior.

Sam was as surprised as the other two that such a huge amount of money was presented to him. His first reaction when told the entire story was that he would like to travel with the trio to Queensland. His wife quickly agreed, saying that it would be nice to spend Adam's first birthday at Brucedale.

The Christmas festivities were as full and exciting for the children as they had always been. James had checked that the celebrations for the Christian holiday were not offensive to Rajiv, knowing he was of a different religion. Rajiv had assured him that he looked forward to the family all being together; he hadn't been in such a large gathering since his first few years in India, when his mother and the Douglases showered him and the other children of the family with the most wonderful gifts they could afford.

Henry had invested in tea and silk and made quite a lot of money in his last few years. Rajiv remembered the 1855 Christmas as one of his favourite times in India.

The Douglas family were all surprised when Rajiv gave each of the children one hundred pounds. He felt very much loved by the children, and the adults treated him as well as any he had ever known.

Chapter 22

IN EARLY JANUARY, Rajiv, Leo and James set off for parts north in hope of finding their lost relations. Sam had wanted to come, but he knew he couldn't be away from the early sitting of the New South Wales Parliament.

They travelled in the new cart Leo had bought some months past. It needed only one horse but was lightweight and travelled well over all kinds of terrain. On reaching Sydney, they decided that the northern railway line would be the fastest way to travel to Casino, where the standard gauge line ended. From that point, they would purchase another wagon for the rest of the journey.

They left the cart with Sam's supervisor. Though only having a meagre thirty acres at Parramatta, Sam was away so often that he needed the man and two others just to keep the farm viable.

Rajiv had travelled many times on railways around England and India, but James had never used anything other than horse-powered vehicles. Leo had, at one time, been in the back seat of the local doctor's Model T Ford for the short journey to Blayney and had vowed never to get inside one of those 'death traps' again. As the train rode on rails, it seemed much safer, though they both still had trepidations.

As the steam got up enough to start the 'red rattler', as they later became known, Leo stood, feeling that he may be sick. After a few miles, when the travel became a little more stable, he felt safer and sat down opposite James. They both watched the passing land with wide-eyed, childlike fascination, and Rajiv smiled to himself, thinking how simple their lives had been.

Casino was a small but thriving town. It had the railway from Sydney and was a meeting point of other inland roads, as well as the costal road through Lismore to Ballina. Lismore was the most populated town in the area, but Ballina was a well-loved fishing port and coastal holiday destination.

They got rooms in a boarding house at Casino, thinking they would rest for a few days. It was obvious that the trip had fatigued Rajiv, and they told the woman who'd answered the door that they would need three beds for at least two nights. The woman was more than happy to accommodate them, until James and Leo returned, carrying the luggage and assisting Rajiv into the front room.

She glared at the three men and, realising that her demeanour had changed, Leo said, 'Is there a problem?' in quite a curt voice.

The woman, looking flustered, said, 'Yes, quite frankly. We do not approve of slavery and will not do business with the likes of you.'

'I am sorry, madam, but it is I who have hired these two men,' Rajiv said, smiling broadly.

'Sir, if that is true, then you are most welcome. We are Quakers here, and this house will not abide with those terrible times when slavery reigned in the land,' she said, taking Rajiv's hand and shaking it warmly.

Leo and James could see the humour in the situation and were even more amused when Rajiv insisted on paying for the accommodation. Once he was safely secured in his room, the two men left the building in search of a cart and horse. There were two livery stables in the main street, and neither had spare vehicles or horses to pull them. Even when they offered a ridiculous amount of money, they were turned away. People heading to the gold field recently discovered near Ballina had purchased all available vehicles. Indeed, for three days, they had no luck in finding the kind of cart and horse they were looking for.

On the fourth morning, a swarthy man of around thirty-five arrived at the boarding house next to theirs. He was tall, and though he was extremely well dressed, he looked out of place and uncomfortable in his suit, fully buttoned shirt and tie.

Leo asked where he'd come from when they met by chance in front of the grand cart in which he arrived. The man answered in an extremely broad accent, saying that he had come from the gold fields and was just staying overnight. His accent was, Leo thought, Scottish, or something like it. He'd had no real dealings with anyone from Scotland, though the doctor's wife back home in Bathurst was similarly difficult to understand. The doctor himself had a strong middle to upper-class English accent, but his wife had come from somewhere in the north of Scotland. At times, when she spoke quickly, Leo could hardly understand a word she uttered.

This man, Joshua Staines, was also quite difficult to comprehend, but Leo gleaned from his prattle that he was heading to Bundaberg on the north Queensland coast, where he had a relatively successful farm on which he grew sugar cane. He'd been to the gold fields to try his luck. Finding that he had none, he was returning home to 'get back to real life'. When Leo heard this, he immediately asked if he and his two friends could travel with Staines to Brisbane.

'That sounds fine. I had to purchase this God-awful trap for a fortune at the diggings when mine was stolen. Damn thieves everywhere, and I had to buy the horse separately. I go home with less money than I came with,' he rambled in his rough brogue. 'Damn the gold. I had a little luck in the first week and thought I would be ready to retire, though I didn't get another strike. Two months digging and nothing to show for it. I don't want to see another shovel in my life.'

Leo thought it hard to understand what Staines meant by being 'ready to retire'. There was no such talk back at Bathurst; everyone worked until they either died or were on the street.

'We'll pay you, of course,' Leo put in. 'We're going to Brisbane to find some relatives.'

'Oh, no, you'd be better off without them,' Staines prophesised. 'They only tax your pocket, and you're stuck with 'em in the end.'

This kind of pessimistic talk wasn't something Leo was used to, and he found it quite strange. He thought the man to be very unhappy with his life. This was, he discovered later, far from the truth. Staines always seemed to put a bad slant on things at the start of a conversation, but really, he thought highly of his family, his 'two wee bairns and the wife'.

'You'll not have to pay. I'll be glad of the company,' Staines continued. 'One man's easy pickings to the riffraff and journeymen around here. You all can be my bodyguards.' He laughed.

Leo hurried back to the rooms and found James and Rajiv in discussion at the table in Rajiv's room. James was in the process of telling him about the waterhole massacre, how the family had come upon the terrible scene back home. They both had tears in their eyes, and Leo waited for almost fifteen minutes until James had completed the story, telling of the baby still clinging to its mother's breast. Leo gave another few minutes out of respect before telling his good news.

'I've got us a free trip to Brisbane,' he announced.

'How'd you work that?' James asked.

Leo beamed, having pulled off quite a coup.

The group met the next morning in front of the second house, with James and Leo carrying all the luggage. The vehicle was a little smaller than they may have liked, with two people in both the front and back. Staines and Sam chatted away up front while Rajiv quickly fell asleep. After an hour or so, James, bored, also drifted into a light sleep. He stirred on every large right-hand bend, as the cart leaned toward the right wheel.

In the early afternoon, the two men up front noticed a rider who'd appeared on the road from the bush. He was too far away to really see, but Staines slowed the horse and reached behind the front seat, taking out a large double-barrelled shotgun.

A second man appeared next to the first. Staines again reached around the seat, withdrew a repeating rifle and handed it to Sam. On seeing this, the two men drifted back into the bush and were not seen again.

'Do you think they were bushrangers?' Sam asked.

Staines shrugged. 'I don't know, but they were up to some skulduggery, or they wouldn't have disappeared. They're not really called bushrangers anymore, but they'll steal anything they can, from your horse to your gold fillings.' He smiled at Sam. 'It never hurts to give a show of strength if confronted by something that makes you feel uncomfortable.'

Sam raised his eyebrows and nodded. Both men continued to hold their guns.

Late in the afternoon, they came upon a small village, which displayed no name sign. A woman and man hurried out from the front veranda of a small but well-kept house and greeted them.

'Looking for a place to stop?' the man asked in a slow drawl.

'Yes, but there are four of us,' Staines answered, expecting to be turned away.

'We can make do,' the woman said. She moved to the back of the cart and began to unload the luggage.

'Let us do that,' James said but was met by a firm hand from the woman.

'Guests don't carry.' She handed the first two cases to a youth who'd arrived from the side of the house.

'That'll be four shillings,' the man said as he began to unhitch the horse. 'The wife's a pretty good cook, and I guess you'll be needin' a healthy feed. Breakfast's included in the morn.'

He led the horse across the road and let him loose in the large paddock beside the house. There was a small but well-tended vegetable garden in the front yard, and all the ground inside the fenced side yard was similarly set to vegetables. No flowers, not one statue or anything to beautify the home. Self-sufficiency was the aim; when there were no paying guests, the family still had to eat.

There was a large hill behind the building, only twenty yards at most from the back door, and no land for farming other than the twenty-by-thirty-yard grounds and the front yard. On the far side of the horse paddock rose sheer granite cliffs of about one hundred and fifty feet. It seemed they were picking a living out of a very small farm wedged between the two precipices.

The boy returned and, when the men had alighted from the vehicle, began to push it around to a gate at the side of the house. He resisted all their attempts to help. On entering the house, they found an extremely neat but tiny main room, where they were proffered the only seats present.

'Thank you for your hospitality, sir,' Leo, the last to take the man's hand, said.

'Well, since I had my accident, this is the only way we can make ends meet,' the man said, without explanation of the accident or his injuries.

'There will be sausages and mashed potato with greens for dinner; I expect you'll want to wash up first. The sink is this way,' his wife said, as she ushered James through the only internal door in the room. It led to the kitchen and a small bathroom.

She pointed to the bathroom and, raising her voice, said, 'The toilet's down in the backyard, so if you need to go in the night, you'll have to take a lantern.'

The kitchen was the largest room in the house; it had a bucket-fed sink and a large table, which could easily seat the family and the four guests. After washing, they were positioned around the table, and a huge loaf of bread was brought straight from the large wood stove and placed in front of Leo. He was handed a serrated knife and, understanding what was expected of him, began to slice it thickly. The woman placed a churn jug of butter in the centre of the unclothed wooden table, and soon, everyone present was devouring the wonderful fresh buttered bread.

The three sausages on each plate were supplemented with a mountain of potato, and great bowls of vegetables were placed in the centre with large serving spoons. The entire group ate their fill, and though Rajiv did not touch the sausages, he'd heaped vegetables on a second plate which he'd requested from the woman.

There was little talk. The meal was magnificent, considering that these people were from humble means, and on leaving the next morning, both James and Staines left healthy tips on the tables next to their beds. All four men had slept in the same room. Three of the four had a less than perfect night, as Staines not only snored as loudly as anybody possibly could, but he also talked in his sleep and appeared to carry on discussions with many phantom callers.

Once loaded on the cart again, the group bid the family farewell and settled into the cross-country trek. Soon, all were asleep except Staines, who whistled and sang with vigour as the miles passed.

The trip to Brisbane from this point was rather slow. The mountainous terrain tired the horse, and though it did not shirk its duties, it still received a tongue-lashing from the driver when it almost stopped while nearing the top of each great hill.

Once in the main streets of Brisbane, most vehicles were motor-driven, and the horse sometimes shied if one came closer than it thought safe. Eventually, they pulled up outside the main post office, and the four said their farewells.

Staines, looking back as he tapped the reins, shouted that they should look him up if they were ever in Bundaberg. They doubted that would ever happen, but none could have realised how prophetic his words were.

Chapter 23

TWO DAYS OF rest were required for Rajiv, and during that time, James and Leo left him in his room at the hotel and started the search for their uncle's family. They began at the courthouse, where births, deaths and marriages were registered, and found that the family home was in a small settlement called Stafford on the north side of the river. They could find no records other than their uncle's death certificate and thought the family must certainly have moved after his death.

They searched copies of the *Brisbane Courier* newspaper after moving to the local library. They found a small story which mentioned William Douglas's death and stated that the family would gather with friends to mourn the passing at 23 Church Street, Stafford. They decided they would visit the home the next day, with Rajiv, and arranged a vehicle and horse from what the sign boasted was 'The largest Livery Stables in the Colony of Queensland!' They had to pay only half what they were asked for when attempting a lesser purchase at Casino.

Early the next day, they left on their journey through the city and the northern suburbs, hamlets, and towns, until they reached Stafford around five in the afternoon. They drove past the small cottage which must've been owned by the Douglas family, and though, on the second pass, James got down and knocked on the front door, there was no sign of life. They decided to find a local establishment to stay at overnight.

James asked one of the few people they encountered where they could find a hotel, and the sprightly old lady, who didn't even stop walking, pointed down the street in the direction in which they were headed, saying, 'Second on the right.'

They pulled up outside the Caxton Hotel a little before dark. The building looked far better from the outside than it did when Leo entered. The proprietor welcomed him and assured him they would be welcome to stay the night, though he only had one room, into which they could place a third bed.

Leo paid the two shillings requested and the three weary travellers retired for a rest until the evening meal, which they were assured would be served at exactly six thirty. Dutifully, they seated themselves at one of the five tables in the dining room and were served a mixed grill. Though Rajiv declined the meat, he was given extra bread and a few vegetables and potato cakes quickly prepared by the cook. This was not fancy food, but they were all hungry and cleaned their plates, much to the delight of the woman who'd served them.

'I like to see a man eat well,' she said, as she collected the crockery and cutlery from the table.

'Yes, thank you, it was very nice,' said James. 'We're visiting from New South Wales and looking for some of our relatives.'

'Well, if they live around here and I don't know them, they must be hermits,' she declared.

'We don't know if they are still in the area. The family name is Douglas.' He thought for a moment, then added, 'They lived at 23 Church Street.'

The woman looked shocked. 'The chef here lives at 23 Church Street. I'm sure that's the number.'

'What's his name?' questioned James excitedly.

'Tom Willis,' she answered, and the expectant faces of the three men fell as they realised that they had probably made a wasted journey and were no nearer to finding the people they were looking for.

'I'll send him in. He might know who owned the house before him,' the waitress said and scurried out of the room.

After a short time, Willis presented himself to the table, wiping his hands down the front of the apron which covered him from neck to knees. It looked as if it hadn't been washed for many days. He thrust his hand at the men, saying, 'I'm Tom. How can I help you?'

'We're looking for our cousins. We aren't sure of their names, but the family name is Douglas,' James said, raising his eyebrows quizzically.

'Yeah, I know the family a little; old Mrs Douglas sold me the home after her husband died. Consumption, I think.' He sized them up one at a time. Realising they were hanging on every word, he added, 'There were two daughters and a son, I think. His name was George. Don't know what the girls were called. The old lady was Grace... No, no, that doesn't sound right. Gertrude. No, I think it was Grace. Anyway, her initial was "G" – that's how she signed the documents when I bought the place.'

Most people didn't pay him much attention, but here he had a captive audience.

'The old lady said they were moving back to where she came from. To her family, like. Now, where did they go?' He thought for a moment, then added, 'You know, I'm not sure, but I think she said Bundaberg.'

The brothers had looked at each other knowingly when the name George was mentioned, thinking of their father. Now, at the mention of Bundaberg, they repeated the glances. If only they had thought to tell Joshua Staines who they were looking for. Surely, he would know all the residents of Bundaberg, where he lived.

'I'm not sure of the place, but I am sure it was north. Pretty sure it was Bundaberg,' Willis stated. Unable to think of anything else to say, he concluded, 'Well, I have a hot stove waiting.' And he left the room, exalted that he was able to solve all the problems which the strangers expressed.

'Looks like we're headed for Bundaberg,' said Leo, and they all nodded.

The next morning, they were out of bed with the rise of the sun. Breakfast was served within an hour, and they were on their way to Bundaberg.

The trip was gruelling. On the first night, they could find nowhere to rent a room, and eventually stopped under a spreading Moreton Bay fig to sleep. This was not a perfect situation for Rajiv. The ground, though it had been covered by a blanket, was still hard and cold. He rose in the morning very stiff and sore. Though he'd never celebrated a birthday, as he had no idea when he was actually born, his two companions were clearly much younger, and had many times slept out in the open. Both looked at Rajiv with worried expressions. When he noticed their concern, he acted as if nothing was wrong.

Later, while he was loading his clothes onto the cart, they spoke quietly, and both agreed that they could not spend another night outside. They feared his health might give out if they didn't look after him. Subsequently, they booked into the first wayside pub they came to and went early to bed after a late lunch.

Rajiv was first to rise in the morning, as if to show he was ready to travel. He knew why they'd stopped the previous day and was determined that he wouldn't be the anchor holding them from their journey.

Travelling throughout the day, they came to beautiful beaches and stopped to bathe at Coolum, one of the most picturesque. The road from here, they learned, went inland for some time, and the hills were quite difficult. Rajiv insisted they continue, and by nightfall, they were in Eumundi. Here, they found a hospitable storeowner who offered them overnight accommodation. Though the rooms were small, the beds were comfortable. The next morning, they ate an early breakfast and headed north again, reaching Gympie late in the afternoon.

Two days later, as they approached Bundaberg, they noticed a familiar horse and cart coming toward them. It was Joshua Staines. He recognised them as they neared and waved frantically.

'What the hell are you doing here?' he questioned loudly as he got down from his cart.

They explained their reason for travelling up from Brisbane, mentioning the Douglas family, and asked if he knew anyone by the name in the area.

'Old Mrs Douglas died about two years ago. Was she related to you?' Staines queried.

'Um, well, yes,' James answered. 'We think she was our aunty–'

Staines immediately interrupted. 'I did know the family a bit. There were a few children, all grown now, though I think the son died soon after they came to live here. One of the girls still lives in the house, or at least nearby.'

They all paused for a moment to think about the ramifications, then Rajiv said, 'We need to visit this place.'

Staines looked at his watch. 'You better turn around and follow me home. It would be too late to bother people by the time we got there.'

'Well, thank you, but we could stay in town,' Leo said, not wanting to impose on Staines's hospitality. They'd already had free travel from him, and Leo wasn't used to taking without paying.

'You'll not be insulting me like that,' Staines said indignantly. Then, as he usually did, he continued, not allowing anyone to answer. 'No, you will be staying with me, and that's a fact.'

Heeding orders, they turned the cart around and followed Staines to his more than respectable home. The seven-bedroom house was, as he explained, an overestimation of the size of the family he and his wife were going to raise. They'd had two children in under three years when first married, and thinking they were going to have a 'large brood', he continued building onto the house. However, his wife had a very difficult pregnancy with their third child and couldn't have further issue.

They were introduced to the family, and Staines explained to his wife and the cook, who was also his mother-in-law, that these good friends were staying a couple of days and would have 'run of the place', as he put it.

A beautiful evening meal was duly served. The two women ate in the kitchen with the children, as there wasn't enough room at the dining room table. Afterwards, they all retired to the spacious lounge room, and Staines lit a cigar. He offered the box of expensive cheroots to his guests, but none enjoyed smoking, and they politely refused the offer.

Staines, like the king of his realm, bade the children goodnight, and soon after, the women also turned in. The men sat for another hour talking over old times. Though they had only met recently, all felt they had a strong bond; indeed, James and Leo kept in contact with Staines for many years after.

Retiring for the night, each was led to an individual room and welcomed the comfort of clean sheets and expensive down mattresses. They all slept well, despite the excitement of the next day's visit, and all three stayed in their rooms until called for breakfast at around eight o'clock.

Travelling into the small town, James was reminded of his childhood, when the city of Bathurst had looked very like the present-day Bundaberg. Similar shopfronts and houses with long, low verandas fronted the main street of the township. He felt, though, that there was greater money here and wondered at the crop, sugar cane, which made it all possible.

With great anticipation, they reached the house expected to be their cousin's. They didn't even know her name. To make the meeting easy, Staines, who had driven them all in his finest carriage, went to the door and asked to see the lady of the house.

The young man who answered said that Mrs Douglas couldn't come to the door anymore, being confined to a wheelchair, but enquired if he could help in any way.

'Who might you be?' queried Staines.

'I'm Edward Douglas, but everyone knows me as George. May I help you?' he answered.

He was bemused by the response this received from the two Douglas men, who had stepped down from the carriage.

'Oh, heavens, we must be your uncles,' James said, stepping forward to shake his hand, followed by Leo. 'We've travelled from New South Wales to meet you and your family.'

'I don't think so,' George said, thinking that these people must be trying to take liberties with the truth, seemingly without purpose. 'My mother only had one sister and two brothers. They've been dead for several years, and none of them had children. My mother's other brother, Edward, for whom I'm named, was lost in the Great War.'

'To hear you say your name was the most wonderful thing. Our father was George Douglas, the brother of William Douglas, your grandfather.'

George looked shocked; he and his mother had thought they had no other living relations. He was a little unsure what to do next when he heard his mother call from inside the house, 'Who is it, George?'

'Um, my mother is fragile, having suffered a stroke about a year ago. I'll have to go in and explain what's happening,' he said, stumbling over the words.

After a few minutes, he returned, saying that his mother would be glad to meet them in the afternoon, as she wasn't currently well enough; she suffered from severe arthritis and anaemia, and hadn't had breakfast. They made a rendezvous point of the only restaurant in the town not connected to a hotel. There was quite a bit of time to waste, and the men decided, under the insistence of Staines, to visit the local shops.

Having filled the back of the cart with provisions for the Staines homestead, and not wanting to wait in the sun, Rajiv, James and Leo walked to the café they were intending to meet at that evening. The proprietor informed them that the establishment wasn't usually open in the evening on a Sunday, but that he would stay if he was assured of a certain income. The agreed price was twenty pounds, and Leo, who'd conducted the business, paid it when they concluded their morning cup of tea.

They returned to the cart and found Staines waiting for them. He had seen the doctor and received some tablets for his rheumatism, and he asked if they would like to accompany him back to the farm or visit Bundaberg's points of interest. Rajiv decided to return with Staines, while Leo and James thought they would have a look around.

Inevitably, they walked around the East Bundaberg Water Tower, which amazed them both. Neither had ever seen such a building. Then they went for a long stroll along Bargara Beach, after a short ride on a hay carter's wagon, which they negotiated for only sixpence each. They walked for a long time on the beach, picking up shells and other curiosities from the sand, until they decided they had better make their way back to town for dinner. They weren't able to find a vehicle for the return journey and so, estimating it to be about ten miles, they began the trek.

At around four o'clock in the afternoon, they reached the town and went to the closest hotel, where they ordered a well-earned drink and used the establishment's convenience to wash and generally straighten up their appearance. By five o'clock, they had seen more than enough of the town for one day and decided they would wait at the café for the six o'clock meeting with their friends and Bundaberg's Douglases. Rajiv, Staines and his wife were next to arrive, and they all partook in a pre-dinner cup of tea.

Six o'clock came and went with the expected visitors not arriving. At six thirty, the party, deciding that the old Mrs Douglas must have been too unwell to attend, began to order their meal from the impatient proprietor.

Around ten minutes later, none other than George Douglas opened the front door of the establishment. He nodded to the table of waiting guests, turned, and backed into the room, dragging an antique wheelchair.

As he neared, all the men stood to greet the splendidly dressed Mrs Douglas. She looked a little uncertainly at the party and raised her eyebrows when she saw Rajiv. She had heard much talk of India and her mother and father's time there but had never seen an Indian man before.

She was a little overwhelmed when they approached, and James introduced them. Shaking the old lady's hand, he said, 'It's wonderful to meet you. I'm James Douglas, and this is my brother, Leo. Your father and ours were brothers.'

Rajiv bowed very low, took her hand and looked into her eyes. 'The likeness is wondrous,' he said. 'You are so like Agnes.'

'I am Agnes.'

Rajiv gasped, and Leo and James shot shocked looks at each other.

'Even your voice,' Rajiv added, surprised. He took the nearest seat, eyes glistening. 'Amazing.'

'I'm at a bit of a loss to understand what you're all talking about. My father thought his brothers to both be dead. One died in India and the other in England. He had contact with only one other relation once in Australia, the cousin for whom I was named, Agnes Douglas.' She paused for a moment, then, seeing their surprised looks, continued. 'Which brother are you supposed to be from?'

'Our father was George Douglas; he was taken to an orphanage as a young child, back in England. He trained to be a cartographer and moved out to Australia at the end of his training,' James explained.

This time, it was the local Douglases who were surprised when they heard the name George.

'Well, I am glad to meet you,' Agnes stuttered, still looking unsure.

'I was in India when your uncle Henry and his family were killed,' Rajiv said. 'Your cousin Agnes was a wonderful friend.' A tear rolled down his cheek. 'I was taken back to England with her, and we lived a wonderful life there.'

'And what has prompted you to come here?' Agnes asked.

'Your cousin had much money and property when she passed away. She trusted me to find her family and distribute the funds.' He sat forward, taking a small piece of paper from his wallet, and said quietly, 'I have a money order here. Agnes asked that it be distributed to her father's brothers or their descendants. As your father's only surviving child, the money is yours.'

Rajiv bent a little closer and pressed the order into her hand. Agnes looked into his eyes for a moment, then unfolded it. 'Oh my God!' she exclaimed. 'This can't be right.' She attempted to pass the paper back to Rajiv, repeating, 'This can't be right.'

He raised his hand. 'Oh, but it is correct. Your father's share of the money is eight hundred and ten thousand pounds.'

With her mouth wide open, Agnes stared at the cheque in wonder. She'd had all three of her children in her forties and lived a frugal life, losing her husband and two eldest children within weeks of each other from influenza. She'd compensated for this loss by guarding her only living son at every point of his life. For the last eight years, she'd been struggling along, making ends meet by doing laundry and creating wedding cakes. She was also a seamstress and would often make the dress and cake for the same wedding.

She gave a little cough and passed the paper on to George. He took it and raised his eyebrows. He'd never thought he would see such a large amount; this was a fortune. He realised his mother was weeping and placed his arm around her shoulders.

'It's alright,' he said, in a calm, soothing voice, and gave her a little squeeze.

'Now I'll be able to put proper headstones on the graves,' she sobbed, referring to the resting place of her husband and their two children.

'Now you'll be able to do anything you like,' George said. He turned to Rajiv. 'Thank you.'

'There is nothing to thank me for. I have but completed the last task set for me by my greatest friend.' He bowed in his usual way of showing respect. James thought how dignified he was and how gentle he had been with Agnes.

Rajiv, James, and Leo told of their lives and the terrible massacres each had experienced in India and Bathurst respectively. Agnes recounted how she'd been married at only sixteen. Her first husband, though a kind man, was an inveterate gambler. He'd disappeared and never been heard of again. She said she always thought some of the people he owed money to had killed him. She'd used their home as a boarding house and, only a few years after her husband's disappearance, had met her second partner, Albert. Though very much in love, they were unable to marry until her husband was legally declared dead. Ten years and three children later, the official death certificate was given, but by then, the children had been christened Douglases, the name she had officially reclaimed.

Agnes and Albert had never married, and then he and the two older children had died. She'd moved George to a friend's home for the three months while she had seen them, one at a time, pass away and arranged each of their burials.

Looking somewhat uncomfortable, she said in a hushed tone, 'George had to be away from the sickness, you see. He was all I had left, and I needed to know he was safe.'

George gave her shoulders a slightly tighter hug, and she went on. 'There was no money left, so I had to work to manage. I was getting nowhere. When a friend of Albert's offered me money for the house, I took the lifeline, and moved home to live with my mother.'

She had begun to speak slower; the stress had tired her. Little more conversation was had as they all ate the excellent food provided. On finishing, Agnes said that they must all come and visit her at home the next day so she could show them family photos.

Dutifully, they came to the house at one o'clock. Staines had dropped them off and gone to town. Agnes, looking much healthier than the previous night, greeted them at the front door. She wasn't in her wheelchair and explained that she only needed it when she was going to have to walk any real distance. She looked years younger, the weight of money worries gone forever.

Agnes told them she'd sent George to the bank to place the money order in her flagging account and that he would return shortly. Prepared on the table were two huge plates of scones, as well as little jam dishes covered by meshed doilies with borders of small beads, which were weighted to keep insects out.

Agnes wore a bright red apron. It had several deep pockets, which carried all of the little knick-knacks she used in everyday life. Her hair was tied back with a matching scarf, and she also wore large red earrings.

The three guests seated themselves, as requested, at the table. Agnes disappeared for a short time and returned with a fresh pot of tea and a bundle of photographs. She untied the bundle and began showing each image, with accompanying stories.

Handing Sam one of the serious-looking pictures, she said, 'That's your uncle William, my father.' She presented the next two. 'My mother and father on their wedding day. This is my brother Edward in his army uniform.'

With great sadness in her eyes, she presented one more of her precious memories, which was a post-mortem photo of William. 'These pictures were popular from the late 1800s,' she said, giving a little shiver.

'Wow, he looks almost identical to our father,' James said and took the next photo, a post-mortem picture of her sister, and then another of her daughter.

'They were very much alike, also,' she said with a quaver in her voice.

Rajiv reached across the table and took her hand. 'And you are so like my Agnes. She truly was the nicest person I ever met.'

She smiled back at him and gave a little nod, then moved her hand away to take the next photo in the pile. James and Leo saw their uncle on horseback and again thought of their father. They saw other members of the family long since departed, and the last image was of Agnes herself with William, leaning on the front gate of the house in Stafford, obviously in happy, contented times.

James talked of his mother and father, saying they would have copies of the family photographs taken and sent to Agnes when they returned home. They wished they had thought to bring some with them, knowing Agnes would see her William in the face of their George.

When young George returned, he told his mother how the banker had almost fallen over backwards when presented with the money order. 'He went a light shade of grey, like he'd seen a ghost.'

Another hour of memories came and went, and soon, the visitors thought they should be on their way to find Staines at the local hotel, their prearranged meeting place. As they said their goodbyes, the old lady kissed her newly found cousins on their cheeks as if they'd always been part of her family life. Then, taking Rajiv's arm, she led them to the front gate and waved until they were out of sight.

George went with them, and the four entered the hotel, laughing about things they'd discussed on their walk. They found Staines a little worse for wear, having spent three or so hours waiting at the bar, drink in hand. He pointed to each in turn to ask what they were having. Pointing to Rajiv first, he received the answer water, and the same from Leo. James and George took a small glass of ale each, and the group settled at one of the bigger tables to discuss the day.

On finishing their drinks, they said farewell to George and mounted the cart.

'I may come and visit you some day,' the young man called as they pulled away.

'We would love to see you, and you would be most welcome,' James called back, and they all waved.

The next morning, Rajiv informed his friends that he intended to get a ship from Brisbane and return to England via India. Strangely, neither had even given a thought to what he would do now that he'd completed his last task.

James said, 'You would be more than welcome to stay at Brucedale.'

'Well, I think the time is right for me to go. I want to make one last trip to India and try to find any of my relations who may still be alive.' Rajiv paused and then added in a nostalgic voice, 'I never saw my father again after we escaped from Cawnpore. He would be well over one hundred if he was still alive. I know he'll be gone, but I may have other relatives, and this is my last chance to find them.'

'I understand,' said James. They had become very close, and neither wanted to say goodbye.

'Actually, there's a ship which comes through Bundaberg and goes to the continent,' Staines put in. 'It starts from Sydney and comes via Brisbane. The only reason it stops here is to take on rum. Our cane makes the best rum in the world.'

'That may even be better,' Rajiv replied. 'The trip on the road takes a lot out of me these days.'

Leo and James looked at each other and raised their eyebrows in a consenting fashion, knowing their opinion wasn't really of any importance.

'If you think that's best, but we were looking forward to having you back at Brucedale,' James said. 'It could be your home, you know. We love having you there.'

Rajiv reached for his hand and shook it warmly. 'I could easily think of you all as family, but I must give finding my own one last chance. Then I must go to London and arrange my affairs.' He took a deep breath. 'I don't have another long trip in me; I'm not the boy I was when Edward and I walked more than a thousand miles.'

He gave a little chuckle and then took Leo's hand and shook it as warmly as he had James's. Leo wasn't good at saying goodbyes, and the words caught in his throat. James put his arm around the two of them, and they enjoyed a hug which was important to each of them.

'I'll go into town and find out about the ship,' Staines said. 'Of course, you two could go back to Sydney by boat as well. There are many ships which do that trip.'

'I'm game, if you are?' Leo said.

'Well, it would be another new experience, and a hell of a lot less work,' James agreed.

'Then that's decided,' said Staines and started to leave the room.

Leo, realising there may be a way he could help, said, 'I'll come with you.' He didn't even wait for Staines to assent but followed him out.

On reaching the town, they travelled a little further, to the harbour. The office where they could book passage was closed, as Staines knew it would be, but he also knew the man in charge of the office and where to find him after hours. He parked the cart, and they wandered over to a small wharf-side café. It was closed also, but Staines knocked loudly, and when there was no reply, he repeated his effort with more vigour.

A large, red-faced woman eventually answered the door and greeted Staines with a curt 'What the hell do you want?'

'Well, hello to you too!' exclaimed Staines in a fake indignant tone.

She relented, realising there was a visitor present. 'Oh, hello, then. What do you want?' she said, only slightly less rudely than she'd started.

'Why, I thought I might find Caldwell here,' he answered and smiled knowingly at the flustered woman. She didn't answer, but said Caldwell popped his head around the door to the residence, which was situated at the far end of the shop.

'We're both closed,' he said, with no pretence of manners.

'I'm sure you wouldn't say that if I was bringing a customer willing to pay an extra ten pounds for the privilege of booking three berths. One to England via India, no less.'

Caldwell, who received a percentage of all bookings from the head office, changed his demeanour with great alacrity. 'I reckon that would make a difference,' he said, in a much more pleasant tone.

'Then you better get that office opened, and we'll make it worth your while.'

Leo smiled to himself. The woman walked away, and Caldwell followed Staines out of the shop. Reaching the gutter, he took the lead, strode quickly to the booking office and unlocked the front door. Though the two men weren't invited in, they followed him anyway.

'I should make you go to the window,' Caldwell said, pointing to the serving aperture. 'However, I think we can overlook that for such important customers.' He knew it would take much more time for him to reopen the window and was hoping to get the men off his hands as quickly as humanly possible.

Caldwell reached for the timetables for ships heading to England. Obviously, the fares to Sydney were of much less importance. 'You're in luck. There's a transport ship due to leave in two days. It goes to England via South Africa.'

'No, sorry, that'll be no good; he needs to go via India,' Leo said, suspecting that Caldwell was just trying to sell the most expensive trip he could.

'You'll need to take a single fare there and then a separate one to England,' Caldwell announced in a disappointed voice. The fare to England would have to be purchased in India.

'When will a ship leave for India?' Leo asked.

'There is also one in two days, but it's a slow old ship, the *Eliza III*.'

'Well, if it's safe, I'll take a first-class berth in the name of Rajiv Arya,' Leo instructed.

'Yes, sir,' Caldwell answered, hardly able to hide his delight; he had not expected to sell a first-class ticket. This would bring him a fine reward. He took a blank ticket from the pile on the counter in front of him and wrote the information required, then rolled the purchase information onto it with a huge stamp.

'That will be twenty-two pounds,' he concluded, reaching out his flattened palm.

Leo withdrew his wallet, took out the required money, and handed it to the greedy little man.

'Thank you, sir. And now, you say you want passage to Sydney?' Caldwell said, taking the money and placing it in the till, which chimed a little bell noise as he closed it.

'I need two tickets,' Leo corrected.

'Well, if you take two single berths, that'll be eight pounds.'

Leo handed it over, and the bell again sounded.

'Will that be all?' Caldwell asked.

'You haven't even told me when the ship leaves,' Leo said.

Caldwell reached for a second, smaller stamp, impressed two tickets and handed them to Leo. 'Three days, every three days, and seeing how you missed today's, you'll have to wait three days.' He looked expectantly at Leo.

Drawing his wallet from his pocket, Staines said, 'It's no good looking to him. It was I who promised you the extra ten pounds.'

He handed the money to Caldwell. This time, there was no sound of the bell, as Caldwell looked at the note and placed it directly into his waistcoat pocket. 'A pleasure doing business with you,' he said, and as they left the building, he added, somewhat sarcastically, 'Please come again.'

Once back in the street, Leo took the last of the money from his wallet and handed it to Staines. 'I'll need to go to the bank and get another five pounds to pay you back.'

Staines looked at his offering and said, with the intention of sounding a little disgruntled, 'I offered the money, and I've paid it.' And he began to walk to the cart.

'But I would like to pay my way,' Leo said sincerely.

'Put your money away, and don't look a gift horse in the mouth.'

'But–'

'We don't need to mention it again,' Staines instructed. He mounted the cart, took the reins and, once Leo had boarded, headed the horse home.

Arriving at the farm, they were met by Rajiv and James, who'd waited for them on the front veranda. Leo presented them both with their tickets and refused to take any money from either of them.

As Leo and James watched Rajiv depart, their distress was evident. There had been repeated farewells, and tears. They knew that they would never see their friend again. He'd had very little to say as they parted.

Dutifully, they waved as his ship left the small dock and headed away. They walked slowly to the café, deciding to have a pot of tea and discuss Rajiv's visit. Both reflected on how much it had changed all of their lives. Not only their money, but the history of their family.

Chapter 24

DULY, LEO AND James enjoyed another visit with Agnes and George, leaving their address and hoping the pair would return the visit. George promised to always keep in contact. They parted in great friendship, and though the brothers never met either Agnes or George again, they did hear that Edward George Douglas met and married Mary Douglas-Godard and started a family with her in Bundaberg. Their firstborn they named Agnes.

Sam Douglas spent another term in government but resigned in 1933 when his attempts to get better conditions for Aboriginal people still fell on deaf ears. He continued to fight for the Wiradjuri when he retired to Bathurst, though almost all of his actions were stymied. He would tell anyone who would listen the story of the Wiradjuri massacre and would always end with the powerful scene of the mother with the baby still at her breast.

James and Leo also told that story and the story of the Bibighar. Their families learned from their many years of storytelling, and could see how much it affected them, even in their old age.

Edward Douglas, Agnes's long-lost brother, was found by Rajiv on his return, through one of his contacts in London. His 'missing in action' letter had been sent to his home in Australia, and though he was later found to have been held in Germany throughout the last two years of the conflict, he was very unwell and for some years was in an asylum in England. Rajiv had distributed all of the money to the Douglases in Australia and so transferred a money order from his own funds to Edward. On a visit to him, Rajiv also passed on his cousin Agnes's manuscript.

Edward attempted to contact his sister Agnes via the address given to him by Rajiv but found that she had died. Though he received one letter from his nephew George, he passed away in 1938 before further contact could be made. He had suffered from dementia but was well cared for by his children, who later contacted the Douglases of Brucedale.

Edward left his home in London to his two sons, twins, George and William. He told stories of the two massacres he'd learned about through Agnes's book to anyone who would listen, though the information was mixed in his mind. His family always listened to the ending and wondered what truth lay in his confused thoughts. It was only when Agnes Douglas's book was found in his belongings that the truth was known.

The families of Sam and James visited the monument at the Bibighar in Cawnpore, India, and the memories of their families echoed in all of their hearts.

The truth of what happened to Jaiemba was never really answered, but Sam and James always held in their thoughts that he had somehow found his people and lived a good life.

The Australian Douglases only once heard of Rajiv Arya again. They were all notified by letter from a solicitor in London that the old man had passed peacefully in his sleep only two years after he'd departed Bundaberg. He'd left his fortune to orphanages in India, except for the house in London, which he left in the name of Agnes Douglas. Douglas House became a United Services Club and served that purpose for many years.

Members of the Douglas family still live in Bathurst, Bundaberg and London today, and the stories of the two terrible massacres, as well as the amazing lives of the family, are still remembered.

The End.

Shawline Publishing Group Pty Ltd
www.shawlinepublishing.com.au